THE HAUNTING OF MURDER HOTEL

A HAUNTING INVESTIGATION SERIES

THE HAUNTING SERIES
BOOK 2

JACK STEEN

ISBN-13: 978-1-987877-98-4 (Print Edition)

WHO WANTS TO STAY AT THE MURDER HOTEL?

First, there was the haunted asylum.

Now, it's a haunted hotel.

I know what you're thinking. Is it really haunted?

Brad says it is. Of course, he's also in prison for the murder of his wife while they were staying at the Brantley Hotel.

As a parapsychologist who studies apparitional experiences, it only makes sense that I check it out, along with the others in my team—Riley and Gabriel.

Gabriel believes Brad. Riley is just excited to stay at a haunted hotel. Me? I think way too many murderers try to claim possession as a way to excuse their actions.

My feelings changed when a ghost attacked me in the bathroom. And then again in my bedroom. And then again during a ritual when we were trying to communicate with the ghost of someone who'd died at this hotel.

Turns out there were a lot of ghosts and a lot of dead bodies.

Keep turning the pages to find out what happens…

NOTE TO READERS

Hey, Confession Addicts!

I figure you picked up this book because of one of two reasons:

One, you've read my confession books and want to give this one a try or…

Two, you like haunted stories and are willing to give this new book a try.

Either way, thanks!

I wanted to try something different, and I hope you like it!

I am working on the next haunting book, so stay tuned.

And yes, to the confession addicts waiting on Book 9 in the Asylum Confession series, I'm working on that too!

To my fellow Asylum addicts in my VIP ADDICTS Subscription group, long-time readers, and to my new friends… Salut!

THANK YOU

Special thank you's to the following "Long Term Patients, Ward Members and Asylum Addicts" from my VIP ADDICTS Subscription. This book would not be possible without your support!

Long Term Patients:
Abi Willshee, Alicatgo, Carissa Clark, Cathulhu13, Chelsea May, Dominique Aragon, Janet Davis, Jayme, Jodi, Kimberly Holland, Kristen Prevendoski, Laura R Hays, Lenora Eagan Bohn, Lola Stracke, Sarah, Sarina Lyn, Steven A Cowles, Taylor Ardwin, Treven Rittenhouse

Ward Members:
Allie Johnson, Amanda Eudy, Andrea, Candice G, Chiffon Cameron, Christine Beam, Constance Gray, Dan, Eryn, Fai Rose, Feyra Stalica, Gaby Lyons, Jen Brooks, Jenna MacDermant, Josh Cummings, Kimberly Kramer, Kymberly Berg, Leslie Weimmer, Luna, Michelle Meyer Stingo, Rachel Miles-Davis, Sarah, Terry Schott, Wendy Elgie

Aslyum Addicts:

Amanda Brand, Amy Keifer, Andrea Buff, Ashley Lewry, Becky
Garland, Dana Cross, Darian, Eric Pokrovsky, Jennifer, Jordan
Hooten, Kelli, Kerra Waldenmyer,
Kristena Hodge, Krystal Walker, Natasha Gray,
Tanya Jack, Taylor Gunter, Terea Rascoe, Tracy Harrison,
Mark Edwards, Valentinova Luttner

These confessions are dedicated to you!

Hell is empty and all the devils are here…

William Shakespeare

CHAPTER
ONE

Ashley's tears mingle with the cold water from the pedestal sink as she splashes her face. The ornate mirror reflects a broken woman, mascara streaking down her skin, framed by the faded grandeur of a clawfoot bathtub and cracked tiles, a bathroom that whispers of past splendor, a time that is now just a shadow.

"Brad, why?" Her whisper is a frail thing, lost in the echo of her sobs.

It's their one-year anniversary, a time meant for celebration, with champagne, laughter, and love. Not this.

This being Brad's venom-tipped words slicing through her heart.

"Bitch, come out." His voice is razor sharp and deep with a darkness she barely even recognizes.

Ashley increases her grip on the edge of the sink, her knuckles pale. What happened to him? Where did this come from?

Everything was fine the night before. They danced the hours away, lost in each other and their love. It was heaven on earth, and things were perfect. They were perfect.

Then, something happened. The change was sudden and unexpected and very unlike the gentle giant of the man she married.

Is it his new medication? The alcohol? The disastrous cocktail has turned their anniversary into a hellscape. Tonight, his eyes, usually so gentle, turned cold and foreign.

"Brad, please…"

His response is a fist thunderous against the wood, threatening to splinter the barrier between them.

She flinches, backing away, her heart pounding in a frantic rhythm. "Please don't break through," she breathes a prayer, her gaze darting to the locked door.

One more hit. Then another one. How many will it take before there are no more chances? She locked herself in the smallest space imaginable, the hotel room bathroom. There are no windows, no escape. She's trapped.

"Please don't do this! Brad, please!" Her voice breaks on his name.

Ashley's gaze shoots to the white marble sink counter scattered with water droplets from her earlier attempts to calm herself. Her heart hammers against her ribcage as she tears through the items lined up like soldiers at attention—soap dispenser, tissue box, a small vase with a single, wilting rose.

"Think. Think," she mutters to herself.

The travel bag huddled in the corner like an abandoned ally catches her attention. She snatches it, the zipper screeching as it gives way to her hurried fingers. The contents spill onto the tile floor, a cascade of toiletries and minor necessities.

"Come on. Come on…" she whispers.

Then, amidst the chaos, the nail file gleams with potential. A small weapon but a weapon nonetheless. Her hand, trembling from adrenaline, clasps the metal file, its pointed tip a shard of hope.

"Open this damn door!" Brad's voice is a battering ram, each syllable a blow against the weakening wood.

Ashley's breath hitches. The door shakes, hinges protesting. She tightens her white-knuckled grip on the nail file, her lifeline in the storm.

"Brad, please, I need you to calm down." Ashley's voice

pierces the pounding silence. "You're scaring me!" Each word quivers as she forces the words out, betraying her terror.

She hates that. Hates feeling weak. She never wanted to be this woman, the kind who cowers, who retreats from a man's rage. She never wanted to be a woman involved with a man who even had rage, which is why she'd fallen in love with Brad. Her gentle giant... yet here she is, confined within four small walls, a barricade against the man she loves and promised herself to a year ago.

"Brad," she whispers more to herself than him, "this isn't you."

Her reflection in the mirror taunts her, a hollow image of a woman who full of strength but shows none. She should fling open the door, confront him, and reclaim her dignity. He's not actually going to hurt her. He never has before.

"Walk out," she urges her reflection. "Just... walk out."

But her feet might as well be set in cement. Fear chains her. Smothers her.

"You're weak, Ashley. Never one to follow through," her mother's voice echoes in the recesses of her mind, haunting her with their accuracy. "All bark. No bite."

"Stop it," she hisses at the ghost of her mother's scorn.

The room feels smaller, the air thinner. Brad's shadow looms under the door, a dark reminder of the barrier between who Ashley is and who she wants to be.

Silence settles like a heavy cloak around her. Ashley holds her breath, listening. The pounding stops.

He sighs, a sound so weary it seeps through the wood. It draws her in, inch by cautious inch, until her ear presses against the cold barrier between them.

Murmurs. Indistinct yet laced with frustration. She strains to catch meaning, her heart pounding a rival rhythm to her earlier pleas.

"I don't want to hurt her." The words slip through, raw and hushed.

Ashley recoils, the nail file almost slipping from her grasp.

Who is he speaking to? Fear twists like a serpent in her gut. His voice, not meant for her ears, carries a secret weight.

"Brad?" she whispers, forgetting herself.

No answer. Did he hear her?

The tile is cold beneath her feet as she backs away, clutching the file like a talisman. He doesn't want to hurt her, so who does? Who is with him? And why?

The murmurs grow louder, more words taking shape.

"She's not like that. You don't know her."

Ashley's frown deepens, etching lines of confusion and fear across her forehead. Her heart skips then races. Who is he defending her to?

"B-B-Brad?" Her voice trembles, betraying her dread. "Who are you talking to?" She raises her voice slightly so he can hear her through the door.

Is he on the phone with someone, maybe? But at this time of night? Panic flutters in her chest like a caged bird seeking escape.

"Brad?" The name comes out sharper and more insistent.

The lack of noise from the other side is thick and charged with an unseen menace.

She needs answers, but the door stands firm between them, both a barrier to the truth and a safety net for her life.

A hushed assertion from Brad pierces the wooden divide. "I'm sure she doesn't think that. She wouldn't do that to me."

Ashley's breath hitches. Her fingers tighten around the cold metal of the nail file. Confusion swirls within her, mingling with creeping dread.

"Brad, listen to me," she calls out, pressing her forehead against the door. "Whatever you think I've done, it's not true."

Bang. Bang. Bang.

Her words feel like whispers swallowed by the growing storm of his rage.

"You just want my money, don't you? Planning to leave me high and dry?" His voice rises, a crescendo of paranoia and anger.

"Brad, no!" Ashley's voice cracks. The room spins, the walls closing in. "That's not who I am. You know me!"

She can hear him pacing, the creak of old floorboards underfoot, his ranting unceasing. But Brad is lost in his own world, a tempest of delusions.

"Please, just stop. Let's talk about this." Desperation paints her plea. "Listen to me!" she shouts, but he is beyond reach, beyond reason.

The door shudders, a splintering crack. Hinges protest. Ashley's heart thunders in her chest. The nail file is slick in her sweaty palm.

"Brad, please—"

The door gives way, crashing inward. Brad, wild-eyed, stands in the doorway, his chest heaving.

Ashley scrambles to her feet, lunging forward, aiming for freedom. The nail file arcs through the air, slashing at him. A line of red blooms on his cheek.

"Get back!" Her voice is sharp, jagged with fear.

He roars—a sound not human—and grabs her, his fingers like iron. He throws her and she hits the ground, her breath punched out.

"Brad, stop!"

But his eyes are alien, frenzied.

Nonsense spills from his lips, garbled words she can't understand. He isn't Brad. Not her Brad. He can't be.

"Please…" she gasps.

His hand holds something. A knife.

"Brad, no!"

Pain. Cold and deep. Darkness edges along her vision, creeping, consuming.

"Brad…" Her whisper fades as the light dims until there's nothing but black.

CHAPTER
TWO

Hannah

Hannah checks her watch for the umpteenth time and rubs the chill from her arms. Seventeen months to the day, there are still moments when she feels the cold presence of the Ghost Lake Asylum's deadly inhabitant clinging to her skin. It always happens when she least expects it, too, like now, when strangers surround her at the Vancouver Airport.

"New beginnings," she mutters to herself, still questioning her decision to move her life from London back to Canada.

She scans the throngs of travelers for Riley's familiar face and pictures him navigating the customs queue, his life packed into a backpack and a metal suitcase, ready to embrace Vancouver's spectral unknowns.

Her own leap across the Atlantic had been a difficult one. She gave up a lot, taking a break from her teaching career and the life she'd made for herself to come back to a place where so many bad memories waited for her.

In the past seven months, she'd been back to Ghost Lake a few times, never voluntarily and never for long. There's no bridge between her and her parents, and she's okay with that. She has to be. Not everyone has that "family weekend dinners and game nights" with their parents, and that's perfectly fine, but she's close now if something happens to them. At least, that's what she tells herself.

Hannah's thoughts drift to Gabriel, whose promises are as insubstantial as the phantoms she hunts. When he suggested Paris, there were seeds of hope that took root in her heart, but it turned out that Paris had only been a mirage, dissolving into a plethora of excuses and disappointment. Gabriel's retreat to his apartment left her stranded in a limbo of what-could-have-beens.

"Change is good," he said, words now echoing hollowly in her memory, as if those three words could erase the destruction of hope that had started to grow.

She once thought there could be something between them beyond coworkers and friends. Now, she knows otherwise. It's a bitter pill to swallow, discovering the man she'd gone through so much with was someone she didn't even know.

Gabriel's nature was, is, and always will be rooted in self-interest.

Following Ghost Lake and the closed door in Paris, Hannah pushed hard to pursue this future. It took some work and a lot of patience, but the government funding finally came through, along with some anonymous donations. There's hope for new beginnings, a future of helping others with her passion and career, which excites her.

"Any minute now, Riley will be here," she whispers as much to herself as to the universe. "And then, we hunt."

Hannah glances at the arrivals board again. A sea of faces blur past her, but she's honed in on only one. Riley. His smile breaks through the crowd like a beacon as he maneuvers his way toward her with a backpack slung over one shoulder and a metal suitcase rolling behind him.

"Hey!" He wraps her in a bear hug, nearly lifting her off the ground.

"Good to see you," Hannah says, relief washing over her. "How was the flight?"

"Madness." Riley chuckles, pulling back. "I sat next to a bloke who wouldn't stop talking about alien conspiracies." He points across the way to a guy pulling a black suitcase peppered with alien stickers.

"It sounds like you had your own paranormal investigation at thirty thousand feet." She laughs, feeling the weight of solitude lift.

They walk side by side, navigating the bustling terminal. In the midst of their conversation, Riley's suitcase hits an uneven tile. It flips and bursts open, and a dozen or so papers scatter like leaves in a gale.

"Damn it," he mutters, dropping to his knees, scrambling to collect his things.

Just then, a woman's high-pitched scream pierces the hum of the airport. They both turn to see a distraught young woman thrashing against two security guards.

"Listen to me!" she wails. "The plane! It's going to crash! I saw it happen!"

"Come on," Hannah says, her voice firm, tugging at Riley's arm as security escorts the woman away.

"Did you hear that?" he asks, his eyebrows knit together in concern.

"It happens more than you'd expect. That was the third outburst I've heard since getting here." She glances at the signs to make sure they are heading the right way. "Let's just get out of here."

The thirty-minute drive from the airport is filled with Riley's excited chatter, something Hannah missed more than she thought possible.

"Check it out, Hannah!" Riley's voice bounces with excitement as Vancouver's skyline gives way to the lush greenery of Kitsilano. "I can't believe you snagged a deal here."

"I can't either. We got lucky, I guess." Her hands are tight on the steering wheel as she maneuvers through the traffic. The ocean winks between the trees, and she can feel Riley soaking in every detail.

"Have you figured out who our mysterious patron is yet? I

mean, they must have some serious coin to cover this, don't you think?" He whistles. "That patron of yours must really believe in ghosts."

"Or in us," Hannah says, though doubt gnaws at her insides.

Living in the Kits is an expensive area. It's a beachside community with adorable boutique shopping areas that are way out of her own personal budget.

Their house looms ahead, its windows reflecting the waning sun. She parks, and they both step out into the cooling air. Riley follows her up the steps, his suitcase clattering behind.

"Well, here we are," she announces, opening the door. "It's not much, but it's home."

"Whoa," Riley mutters, surveying the chaos within. Books are piled high, papers are strewn across the floor, and boxes clog the space. "You know, this reminds me of your office back in London." His eyes twinkle as he gives her a cheeky grin.

"I did kind of clean," she tries to joke. "I've been a little... busy, I guess?" She knows her smile doesn't quite reach her eyes even though she tries.

"Nightmares again?" Riley's tone is gentle and observant.

"Jake isn't resting," she admits, avoiding his gaze.

After Ghost Lake, she confided in both Riley and Gabriel about Jake's visits. Between the two men, Riley seemed to be the one who understood the most, which surprised her at the time. Now, not so much.

"Damn." Riley runs a hand through his hair, concern etched on his face. He bends down, opening a box labeled "EVP Recorders."

She's thankful he doesn't ask questions or try to prod for more information. For a chatterbox, he knows when to stay silent.

"Any jobs lined up yet?" He pulls out a tangled mess of wires and makes a note on his phone.

"Too early," Hannah says, watching him work. "Someone will bite, though. I know it."

He drops everything to the floor and gives her a solid look. "Did I just uproot my life for nothing?"

His question hangs in the air between them.

It's a good question—a solid question—that deserves an answer that has eluded her for a long time.

She digs in deep and lets the answer come without any thought. "Never," she says with a firmness that even surprises her. "We have funding, remember? We just need to spread the word."

Riley scoffs. "You know, I kind of figured Gabe's book would've thrown us a bone."

"You and me both," Hannah murmurs, thinking of Gabriel's silence.

Following Ghost Lake, Gabriel retreated to write a fictionalized version of their experience there. Like a frenzied man, he wrote it within a few months, and his publisher picked it up, rushing it through the publishing process, which apparently was highly unusual.

"Well, he's not here, but we are, and that's what matters." He stands to his feet, hands on his hips. "The first thing we need to do is get organized while I'm still awake," Riley says, determination replacing his earlier doubt. "We'll make this work."

"Right," Hannah agrees, her own resolve strengthening now that Riley is here. They are in this together, no matter what haunts them.

CHAPTER
THREE

GABRIEL

Gabriel Ambrose stands at the heart of the crowded Parisian bookshop, his deep voice barely making a dent in the packed room as he reads a short piece from his book, picking a section from the chapter where he met the evil spirit that resided in Ghost Asylum. His words are flamboyant and filled with fervor, and the way he over-exaggerates specific sections only adds to the horrific setting he wants to impose. The crowd eats it up.

The man he is now is a reflection of the man he used to be, a man the audience remembers, and a stark contrast to the grim tales that haunt most of his waking and dreaming moments.

The crowd hangs on to every anecdote, and an occasional knowing smile emerges among those familiar with his work. He's in his realm once again. He knew he missed it but didn't realize how much.

"*Et voilà,*" he concludes in French, his accent charmingly imperfect.

The room erupts in applause, a sea of adoration washing over him.

His gaze flitters about, taking in the faces until he stops at one who stands there unmoved, a young woman, her intense scrutiny seeing more than it should. Her hands are clasped in front of her, a large diamond ring resting on her finger.

Gabriel meets her gaze, and for a moment, the clamor, the noise all around him, dims.

"*Merci beaucoup*," he says, nodding graciously to his fans, knowing he's butchering the French language with his British accent. The showman in him drinks in the praise, yet the woman's stare lingers like a haunting shadow.

"*Pour vous, Madame*," Gabriel flirts with an older admirer, signing her book with a flourish.

Everything is going well until he looks across the room, searching and finding her—the solemn woman, hands twisting together as if wringing out a secret or, at best, trying to make a decision.

Whatever it is she's wrestling with, he hopes it has nothing to do with him.

He waits until the line is cleared before he leaves his seat. What he wants to do is shake hands with the bookstore owner and leave, but instead, he finds himself making his way toward the woman still standing in the corner, surrounded by shadows.

"Is everything all right?" Gabriel asks her, feigning nonchalance.

"Just... thinking," she murmurs, her voice barely audible as she lightly touches his hand.

A sharp pain pierces Gabriel's head. Visions flash in front of him—blood smeared across wooden floorboards, an outstretched hand, a silver ring catching the light from a lifeless finger. A shooting pain with the speed of a falling star tears through him, and he staggers backward, his arms reaching out for something to hold on to.

"Gabriel? *Mon ami*, are you okay?"

The bookshop owner's hand on his shoulder brings him back. Gabriel blinks, disoriented, glancing up at the faces around him, all pinched with worry. He's on his knees, and the signing table is now a lifeline. How did he get here when he was...

He twists toward the corner where he just stood, but the woman is gone.

"*Je suis désolé*," he stammers, pushing himself upright.

Everyone is staring at him, their gazes pinched with concern. The person he doesn't see is the woman who reached out and touched him, evoking the vision. Where did she go?

"I am so very sorry, but I must cut this short."

"Of course. Of course. Let me help." The owner quickly places Gabriel's pens and business cards into his bag and pushes the rest of the unsigned books to the side. "Perhaps you can come back tomorrow to sign these? I have customers who have special ordered them."

Gabriel nods, willing to agree to anything at this point, and hurries outside.

Gabriel's fingers fumble with a pack of cigarettes as he walks down the rain-slicked cobblestones. The bookshop's warm glow fades behind him, replaced by the chill of a Parisian evening. He lights a cigarette and inhales deeply, the smoke mingling with the misty breaths of the city.

"Damn it," he mutters to himself. Of all nights for something to happen, why tonight?

He hails a taxi to take him back to his flat, the same flat he has been trying to sell to pay his outstanding debts, but no one is biting. He never should have offered it to Hannah last year.

Hannah.

Simply thinking of her floods him with tremendous guilt. She was the one good thing in his life, and he pushed her away. He should have told her the truth from the very beginning. He hated lying to her, and he hates that he's still doing it. His pride and his embarrassment are too much, too overwhelming for him.

He knows what she thinks of him. He hates that she believes it too.

He almost told her the truth when he'd last been back in London. He managed to sell his measly flat there to cover his debt to Sharps, and after signing the paperwork and handing over the keys, he found himself standing outside her office, staring up into

25

the darkened windows. If there'd been a light on, he would have walked up and confessed everything. Instead, he took it as a sign that he should leave her life.

It was cowardly, but facing her disappointment is something he's not sure he can handle. He couldn't then.

He still can't.

As a taxi pulls up, a hand on his arm startles him. It's her, the woman from the signing. Her eyes are dark pits of exhaustion, rimmed with haunting shadows.

"Mr. Ambrose. I think I need your help," she says, her voice steady but revealing an undercurrent of desperation.

"Look, I'm not—" he says, stepping back, but something about her plea pierces through his fatigue. He keeps his hand on the passenger door handle, but for some reason, he doesn't pull to open the door.

"I read your book. What you did for that woman…" she trails off as if the words are stones too heavy to carry. "Tell me, do you truly believe evil spirits can possess places?"

Ghosts. Spirits. The memories of the Asylum claw at his conscience.

Gabriel exhales a cloud of smoke and nods. "Yes, I believe it. I've seen it. I've survived it."

"Good. I need that belief." She nods a few times, glancing off into the distance. "I'm pretty sure my brother-in-law was possessed by an evil spirit and killed my sister."

Her words hang between them, cold and sharp. The cigarette nearly slips from Gabriel's fingers. Her revelation echoes in his mind, a chilling reminder of the forces he knows all too well.

"I'm very sorry to hear that, but there is nothing I can do," he tells her, his response on autopilot even though everything inside him yells the opposite.

Of course he can help her. That's why he wrote the book—to prove he's not a washed-up medium—but offering to help means contacting Hannah, and he's not sure he's ready to do that.

Maybe once everything is taken care of here, when he's closed this chapter of his life and can start fresh, he can be the man Hannah needs him to be.

It's a big maybe, but miracles do happen, right?

"Please," the woman begs. "We need your help." She slips a piece of paper into his jacket pocket before she steps back from the curb. "We will pay you," she says as if that one little detail will make all the difference.

The taxi driver honks, and Gabriel pulls the door open and ducks his head to enter. It's not until he's given the driver his address that he pulls out the piece of paper and finds both a phone number and email address written down along with a price they're willing to pay.

He gulps. When the woman said they could pay, he hadn't expected this. This price would mean he wouldn't need to sell his Parisian flat, even with sharing it with Hannah and the kid. He could become that man he knows he can be.

He could try to win Hannah back.

CHAPTER
FOUR

HANNAH

Hannah's heels click on the polished floors of the University of British Columbia's Psychological Sciences Building as she approaches the dean's office. The air is sterile, and the fluorescent lights above flicker ever so slightly, casting an unsettling pall over the corridor.

Breathing in deep, she gathers her courage, reminds herself she's someone to be listened to even if people don't know it yet, and knocks.

"Come in," the muffled voice from within calls out.

"Dean Richards," Hannah says as she walks in and closes the door behind her, "thank you for meeting with me."

He peers over his glasses, a thin smile not reaching his eyes. "Ms. Wilkins, I must admit your resume is… unique."

"Thank you, sir. I assure you my lectures on paranormal psychology bring a fresh perspective to—"

"Paranormal?" The word drips like sour candy from his mouth. "I've read your commendations from London University, but here at UBC, we pride ourselves on empirical evidence."

"Sir, there is evidence—" Hannah protests.

"Have you considered Vancouver Community College?" he

interrupts, waving a dismissive hand. "Your... 'expertise' may fit better there."

"Sir, I—"

"With respect, I don't want to waste your time or mine, Ms. Wilkins, so let me be clear. Your area of study is not one that we..." He hums and haws for a moment, as if trying to find the right wording. "...accept as serious, as of yet."

As of yet. At least he's giving her that.

Hannah simply nods, not finding the words to argue. "I appreciate your time, Dean Richards."

As she leaves his office, she catches the sound of his disdainful sniff echoing off the cold walls.

"What an ass," she mutters once the door closes behind her.

She came here anticipating skepticism, but the weight of it still stings. She shouldn't be surprised, not really. It would be difficult for most of her colleagues to take her seriously and that it would be a struggle to get this new business off the ground, but she didn't think it would be *this* hard.

It's even a struggle with the police. Despite their help in Ghost Lake, the department there was more than happy to brush everything under the rug and disregard the reality of what happened, which, to be honest, hasn't helped with people's skepticism.

Her encounter with the police chief yesterday flashes in her mind, a stark reminder of the uphill battle she is facing.

She met with the Chief of the Vancouver Police Department, offering their services for the difficult cases that can't be explained. It had been a long shot, sure. The only reason she even managed to secure that meeting was because the chief's wife is a fan of Gabriel's, having read all of his books. Hannah basically had to promise a personal visit from Gabriel whenever he comes to visit.

The chief made it very clear that, from one professional to another, he was disappointed that she would think he'd even consider working with her. He all but called her a con artist, preying on weak people's superstitions and delusions. The meeting lasted only ten minutes, but she'll never forget how degraded she felt walking away.

Not paying attention to her surroundings, Hannah collides with a figure emerging from the shadows. "Sorry," she says before recognizing the woman from the station yesterday. "Detective Cho."

"Please call me Jenny. Rough meeting?" she asks, a hint of sympathy in her eyes.

"Something like that." Hannah tries to mask her frustration.

"Here, let me get you a coffee." Jenny gestures toward the vending machine, its hum oddly loud in the otherwise silent hall.

"Thanks," Hannah says, accepting the steaming cup.

Jenny leans against the wall, sipping her own drink. "I heard some of what was said yesterday." She gives Hannah a small shrug. "My desk is the closest to his door, so he can keep an eye on me."

A secretive smile plays on her lips, and Hannah isn't sure if it's because she enjoys keeping the chief on his toes or if it was over what she heard.

"My grandmother was superstitious," Jenny continues. "Korean folklore and spirits were part of my childhood."

"Really?" Completely intrigued, Hannah hands the detective her card. "Let me guess. Some of that gets you in trouble at work?"

The detective's smile grows. "Vancouver has the second largest Korean population in Canada, so whether the chief likes it or not, dealing with superstition is part of the job." She holds out her own card, which Hannah takes. "Listen, I can't promise anything, but if something… weird comes up, I'll be sure to give you a call."

"Thank you, Detective." Hannah tucks the card away.

Maybe things won't turn out so bad after all.

When she returns home with coffee she'd picked up from a shop just down the street, Hannah pushes the door open. Not for the first time, she winces as it creaks. It sounds like a groan coming from the depths of an ancient crypt, and she mentally kicks herself for not getting some oil and fixing the hinges.

Stepping into the dimly lit living room, Hannah's shadow stretches out, stitching across the floorboards to where Riley sits, surrounded by scattered papers.

"Riley, what's all this?" she asks, navigating through the chaos. Then, she hands him a coffee.

"Potential cases," he says, his voice a mix of exhaustion and excitement. "I figure there's got to be a job in here somewhere. I've made a few stacks, separated by region and then by the paranormal anomalies." He gestures toward the methodically sorted piles, his pride in the organization apparent despite the disarray.

Hannah picks up a handful of articles from the "ghosts" stack and skims the headlines. *Eerie Laughter in the Attic, Phantom Footsteps on Route 66, The Weeping Woman of Willow Creek.*

She raises an eyebrow, impressed. "You've been busy."

"We both need to do our parts. You're holding the meetings, what with the police yesterday and then the university today. The least I can do is put in some time and do some research. Oh, I, uh, used up a lot of your printer ink and didn't know if you had more on hand or not, so I ordered some. Hope that's okay." He shrugs before taking a sip of his coffee. "Bloody hell, what is this stuff? Liquid gold?"

"Good, right? There's a coffee shop just a few blocks down." She plops down on the couch and looks over what he printed. "Anything of interest yet?"

"There's some promise in the ghost pile. Some local stuff, too, and by local, I mean within an eight-hour drive north from here, which is crazy because that's like driving from London to Frankfurt. Canada is huge, man."

She smiles faintly, still feeling the sting of the day's rejections but appreciative of his dedication and excitement. "It's too nice of a day to waste indoors. Let's take these outside," she suggests, picking up the ghost pile from the floor.

A few minutes later, they settle in the yard, the golden hues of sunset painting their makeshift workspace. The soft rustle of paper dances together as they work through the pile together, sifting stories of spectral encounters from potential hoaxes.

"Look at this one," Riley says, holding up a particularly lurid headline. *"Ghost Bride Haunts Honeymoon Suite."*

She glances at it quickly. "Too tabloid," Hannah says. She finishes her coffee. Are you getting hungry yet?" The look he gives her has her chuckling. "Why don't you come in and help make dinner then? I've got the makings of a great stir-fry if you're up to it."

"Um, Hannah, no offense, but how about I cook while you sip wine and chop the vegetables? I've had your cooking before, and, um…" He lets his voice trail off, not bothering to say what they both know. She's a horrible cook.

She grabs the stack she was working on and holds it tight to her chest. "Listen, just because I'm a woman doesn't mean my place is in a kitchen, and I'll have you know, I'm very skillful at knowing the best restaurants to order from."

"Still, the stir-fry sounds good, as long as you are my sous chef. You chop. I'll create."

She smiles, enjoying their camaraderie. Even though Riley has somewhat of a crush on her, they make a good team.

"Sounds good. After dinner, I'll start digging into some of the names in these pages," she suggests.

She turns to find a shape looming from the dark edge of the porch. The papers she's holding fall to the ground as she recoils, heart hammering, a gasp caught in her throat.

CHAPTER
FIVE

"What the hell?" she blurts out.

Talk about hammering hearts. Hannah feels like hers is about to burst from her chest.

"Hey, just me." Gabriel stands there, arms held upright, one bag casually slung over his shoulder while a few others sit at his feet.

"Jesus, Gabriel!" she exclaims, bending down to gather up Riley's printed research. "Don't do that!"

Gabriel chuckles. "Sorry, Hannah. I see you're still jumping at shadows."

"Should have known you'd be the one lurking in them," she retorts.

Relief quickly smooths the crease of fear from her brow. She doesn't know how she feels about him showing up like he has, out of the blue, with no word.

"Hey, Riley," Gabriel says, reaching for Riley's hand in a firm shake. "Read your book on the flight over. You've got quite an imagination."

"Thanks, I think?" Riley replies, clearly unsure whether to be flattered or offended.

Hannah looks from Riley to Gabriel and back to Riley. She

knew he was writing a book but had no idea he finished it or that he sent it to Gabe to read. She feels left out, and that bothers her.

"You're done? I'd love to read it," she tells him.

When Riley's face blazes beet red, she understands why he hasn't said anything yet. He probably wants to make sure it's perfect before giving it to her.

"Another round of editing, and it should be good to go." Gabe continues, the teasing glint in his eye unmistakable. "But it's all about selling the sizzle, right?"

"Definitely," Riley says. "You didn't think it was too over-written?"

Gabriel shakes his head. "You've got the wow factor. Throw in as many twists and turns as you can to hook the reader. If it's a little overwritten, you can fix that in edits."

Riley's brows lift. "Yeah, okay. Well, I figured if anyone would know about pushing the limits and overwriting, it would be you."

The dig hits its mark as Gabriel quickly glances away.

There's an obvious tension in the air that Hannah doesn't like. "So, what brings you back from Paris?" she asks.

Gabriel turns to meet her gaze. There's a lot he doesn't say and a lot he obviously doesn't know how to say if the way he opens and closes his mouth is any indication.

It's unlike Gabriel to be at a loss for words, and Hannah isn't sure what to make of that. Does she forgive and forget or force them to communicate and deal with what could have been between them?

"Found us a case." Gabriel's tone shifts, the moment gone. "A real intriguing one, about a sister, a husband, and a ghost."

"Hmmm. Well, at least you're pulling your weight." Sarcasm drips from Riley's words.

"Riley," Hannah cautions him. "Play nice."

"It's fine, and I get it, but I'm here with a case. Listen, can we go inside to discuss?" Gabriel motions toward the house. "This one's… different."

The three of them head inside, the air thick with the promise of untold horrors and the thrill of the hunt, a feeling she hasn't felt since… well, since Ghost Lake. The weight of the day's skepticism lifts, replaced by the familiar, electric charge of possibility.

Gabriel drops his bag on the floor and hands her one of the bags he's holding. "I picked up some wine and cider. Hope that's okay?"

"Wine? Where's the whiskey?" Hannah asks, eyeing the bottle and appreciating the label. It's one of her favorites but also expensive.

"Trying to lay off the hard stuff for a bit," he says as Riley hands him a corkscrew.

Hannah waits until he's filled three glasses before she breaks the silence. "Okay, spill it," she says, her voice a mix of skepticism and curiosity.

"Her name's Andrea," he begins, his eyes reflecting a seriousness that draws them in. "She was at a recent book signing and quite insistent I hear her story."

"In Paris?" Hannah asks.

"About her sister?" Riley follows up, not giving Gabriel a chance to answer.

"Yes, the signing is in Paris, but her sister isn't. Or wasn't. She was murdered," Gabe confirms with a nod, "by her husband, Brad. At The Brantley Hotel, San Diego."

Riley whistles.

"San Diego? That place has some dark history they try to keep quiet," Hannah muses. "Why was her sister in Paris, though? Just to meet you?"

"Her sister wasn't. Andrea was," Gabriel says. "That's not important, though. What is important is that Andrea's sister and her husband were at the hotel to celebrate their first year anniversary. They were supposed to be lovebirds or something like that."

"Supposed to be?" Hannah arches an eyebrow.

"Best friends turned lovers. He is a high-flying CEO. She was a nurse. They met after a cycling accident that had him in the hospital. Picture-perfect romance from what Andrea says."

"Until murder joins the party," Riley quips dryly.

"Exactly." Gabriel's voice falls flat. "Andrea swears Brad

adored Ashley. She said he wouldn't hurt a fly, let alone kill his wife. In all the years they'd been together, Andrea had never seen Brad get angry. Apparently, they were soulmates."

"Give me a break." Hannah scoffs. "Nothing is perfect, not people, not relationships, not anything. He probably had everyone fooled."

"Or possessed, according to Andrea," Gabriel adds.

"Come again?" Hannah frowns, leaning forward.

"Classic defense," Riley states. "Demons made me do it."

Hannah gives Riley a look. She can't tell if he believes it can happen or finds the idea ludicrous.

"Andrea believes it. Deeply."

"Did you tell her we aren't police detectives?" Hannah asks, wanting to make sure she knows everything about this story Gabriel is presenting.

He nods. "She says the police laugh whenever Brad says an evil spirit possessed him."

Hannah's not sure if she buys it, but she is intrigued. "Lots of murderers claim they were possessed. BTK claimed he was when he killed ten people. And..." She glances first at Riley then Gabriel. "...we don't really deal with demon possession."

Gabriel gives a slow nod. "True, but I think this is different. He swears he does not know about the murder. All he recalls is that he heard voices in the hotel room right before he blacked out. When he woke up, he was on the floor beside his dead wife, knife in hand. He gave himself up willingly."

Riley leans back in his chair, almost to the point of tipping over. "So what makes this case so intriguing to you then?"

"The hotel's past. I did some digging into the hotel, and it has quite the history of murder and tales of ghostly sightings, something we do deal with," he says directly to Hannah.

She doesn't reply.

"The most famous possible murder in the hotel was Darla Hopkins in 1925. Her new husband was a very rich and powerful man, and while he went to meetings and such, she stayed in the hotel. No one ever saw her leave their room, but her husband claimed she ran away with a large sum of his money. Not long after, he was found dead in his hotel room, poisoned."

"Karma?" Hannah suggests.

"Maybe. One of the hotel maids ended up confessing. She says something made her poison the man after she saw him kill Darla and hide her body in the walls of one of the rooms. Guess which floor?"

"Thirteenth floor?" Riley offers.

Hannah shakes her head. She's not sure if she's buying it or not. "Convenient number for a ghost story."

"Do some research, and you'll find it's more than stories."

Riley is humming in his seat. He's playing with the wine glass, twirling it round and round on the table. "Did they find the body?"

Gabriel shakes his head. "The police, of course, didn't believe the maid, but the hotel owners ended up sealing the thirteenth floor after that."

"What happened to the maid?" Hannah asks.

"She was executed, but here's the interesting part. There have been multiple sightings of her in the hotel."

"What about Reginald Hopkins? Any sightings of him since he was killed in the hotel too?" Riley questions.

Gabriel shrugs. "Not that I could find. I read a couple accounts of flickering lights and cold spots on both the twelfth and fourteenth floors, but all sightings have been of the maid. No one else."

Hannah taps her finger on the table, taking it all in. Gabriel's right. This is up their alley, and who doesn't want to go to San Diego?

"I'll see what I can pull up tonight," Riley offers. He turns to Hannah. "I'm kind of liking it, though. Sounds too good to be true. I mean… this is what we do, right?"

Hannah smiles at him. "Did you get a physic reading from the woman in Paris?" she asks Gabriel.

"Sort of," he hedges. "She touched my hand, and I saw images of blood and a blond woman on the floor before we talked. She showed me photos, and her sister was blond."

Hannah keeps tapping her finger on the table. "And you believe her?"

He hums and haws, looking everywhere but at her. "Well, she's paying us to look into it," he finally admits.

Hannah stops the tapping. That's why Gabriel is here. Not because of her or Riley or anything else but because there's money involved. Just like with Ghost Asylum.

"It's starting to sound like our kind of job," Riley adds his own two cents to the conversation, either not reading the room or ignoring it.

"Haunted hotel, tragic love story, possible possession…" Gabriel trails off, watching Hannah closely.

"Fine," she exhales, the word more surrender than agreement. "We'll look into it."

"Good." Gabriel smiles. "Because if there's even a shred of truth to it…"

"We'll find it," Riley finishes as the dying light cast long, creeping shadows across the room.

CHAPTER
SIX

The cottage, though quaint, now feels oppressively small, every corner filled with unresolved tension.

In the dim light, the king-size bed in Hannah's room looms, seemingly larger and more imposing, a reminder of both comfort and the uneasy situation. She slides beneath the cool covers and glances over at Gabriel, who has settled himself on the floor with a thin blanket for cushioning. Every time he shifts, she hears the faint groan of his discomfort and guilt gnaws at her.

She could offer to switch places. In fact, she probably should.

But she doesn't. She doesn't want to sleep on the floor, either.

Finally, after listening to him toss and turn, sighing in frustration, she snaps. "Can't you just… get up here?"

The words come out before she can reel them back, surprising even herself. She meant to send him to Riley's room even though there's only a double in that one.

"Are you sure?" Gabriel's voice carries a note of hesitation, yet there's unmistakable hope there too.

"Get up here before I change my mind," she mutters, feigning irritation to mask the odd sense of anticipation twisting in her chest.

With a grunt, Gabe climbs into the bed and settles next to her. The silence stretches, both of them lying stiffly on their respective sides, an invisible barrier—and one strategically placed pillow—keeping them apart.

Hannah stares hard at the ceiling, her fingers clenching the sheets. The old, familiar ache of attraction rises, and she hates herself for it. She's better than this. She's a grown woman who knows better than to let this past connection tangle up her emotions again.

"I—" Gabriel starts, breaking the silence.

Hannah immediately turns her back to him. "Goodnight," she cuts him off, closing her eyes against the memories and feelings that threaten to resurface.

She focuses on her breathing, blocking out his faint presence beside her, and slowly, eventually, she slips into sleep.

But her dreams are dark and twisted, pulling her into a nightmare as vivid as the present. She's in a hotel room, shadows clawing at the walls. The smell of blood hangs thick in the air. On the floor, blood smears across the carpet, dark and ominous. A young woman lies on the bathroom tiles, her face pale, eyes wide with horror. Her mouth moves soundlessly, forming the words, *"Help me."*

Hannah jerks awake with a strangled gasp, her body cold and drenched in sweat.

Gabriel is instantly there, his arms wrapping around her before she can fully orient herself, his strength steadying her against the wave of terror threatening to drown her.

"Let go!" she protests, trying to pull away, but her hands tremble uncontrollably. Her mind is still half-ensnared in the nightmare, echoes of that helpless young woman's eyes haunting her.

"Shh, it's okay," he murmurs, holding her tight. His voice is a balm against the lingering nightmare, grounding her back in the present.

She resists at first, struggling against his hold, but he doesn't let go. The trembling subsides, her heart rate slowing as she breathes in the warmth and safety of his embrace. His hold is firm and unyielding. Bit by bit, the remnants of fear loosen their grip on her.

After a moment, he releases her, leaning back. "Do you want to talk about it?" he asks gently.

She hesitates, fluffing her pillow as she buys herself a moment to gather her scattered thoughts. "It was just a nightmare," she whispers finally.

"About Jake?" he asks, his voice soft.

Hannah goes still. Slowly, she realizes with a shock that, for the first time, it wasn't Jake haunting her dreams. In fact, he's been quite absent lately. Strangely, she thinks she misses that.

She glances around the room, almost expecting to see some shadow of him lurking, but there's only Gabriel, his eyes watching her with gentle concern.

He's gone.

Jake's gone.

The enormity of it swells within her, and she feels a prickling behind her eyes as a wave of emotion rises, thick and unexpected. She closes her eyes, feeling the hot tears press against her lids. It's an alien relief, and yet it terrifies her. How can something that defined her for so long simply vanish without her noticing?

"What was it about, then?" Gabriel's voice pulls her back, soft and curious.

She swallows hard and reaches for the glass of water on the side table. She takes a slow sip, letting the cold water soothe her parched throat. "I was… in a hotel room," she begins, her voice trembling slightly. "There was blood. So much blood. A young woman on the floor. She looked at me, and she whispered, 'help me.'"

He listens intently, nodding as if he understands more than she says. "I've had a similar dream. Or vision, maybe." He pauses, glancing at her with a mixture of resolution and concern. "I think… I think we really need to check that hotel out."

The way he says it and the steady resolve in his voice has her chest tightening. It feels like he's offering her a lifeline into a future she never dared imagine.

He opens his arms, his silent invitation both comforting and tempting.

Without a second thought, she leans into him, resting her head on his chest, feeling the rise and fall of his chest. His arms circle her, drawing her close, and she lets out a sigh as the tension of the night begins to dissolve.

His heartbeat is steady beneath her cheek, a gentle reminder that, no matter the ghosts they chase or the nightmares they face, she isn't alone.

For the first time, she dares to believe that maybe, just maybe, she can let herself be safe here—in his arms, in this fleeting moment where past and future collide, and hope feels real.

CHAPTER
SEVEN

The old diner's neon sign buzzes, casting an eerie glow on the rusted pickup trucks in the gravel lot. Hannah steps out of the rental car, the chill of the evening wrapping around her like a shroud. She didn't realize just how cool California could be in the evenings. When she agreed to fly to San Diego with Gabriel to meet Andrea, she didn't realize Andrea lived about forty minutes east from the city in a small town called Flinn Springs.

Of all the places to meet, why did she have to pick an old diner like this one? Most likely, Andrea doesn't want anyone to know of this meeting, but why this particular place?

The air is thick with the scent of stale coffee and fried food, and a quiet hum of a forgotten song plays on the jukebox. Hannah follows Gabriel as he heads toward the back to a corner booth where a small woman sits, her hands clasped tightly around a chipped mug.

"Thanks for coming." Andrea's voice trembles. Dark circles etch beneath her eyes like bruises.

Hannah slides into the seat opposite her, the vinyl cracking under her weight. "How have you been holding up?" Her voice is soft, but in the diner's silence, it feels invasive.

"I haven't been sleeping well." Andrea's words spill out, raw and edged with fatigue. She glances over at Gabriel then quickly looks away.

"I understand," Hannah says, filling the silence. "All of this must be so hard."

"Why are you convinced that your brother-in-law didn't do this?" Hannah's question is punctuated by the clink of her spoon against the mug as she stirs sugar and cream into the thick sledge. She should have just ordered a soda.

Tears shimmer in Andrea's eyes. "I wasn't at first... I was devastated when I got the news. It was like losing them both. And of course, I was angry. Who wouldn't be? I wanted him to pay for what he did, but then..." She pauses, her gaze dropping to the hands and sighs. "When I saw him in court that first time, all I could remember was the sweet, loving man that Ashley fell in love with. My sister wouldn't fall in love with a murderer. She couldn't have, and then, in that courtroom, he was so deflated and haunted." She looks up. "He cried through most of the trial."

"Guilt can do that to a person." Hannah's skepticism remains veiled behind a mask of concern.

Andrea shakes her head. "No, you don't get it." Her fingers tap an anxious rhythm on the table. "The man I knew and the monster they're making him out to be, they're two different people. I needed to know, even if it was going to kill me, so I went to the prison to visit him."

Hannah glances at Gabriel, surprised at his silence. There's a compassionate look on his face as he stares at Andrea. What hasn't he told her about his time in Paris? What else did he see when Andrea touched him that he's keeping to himself?

"He's lost so much weight. His clothes just barely hang on him. He's so depressed all he does is cry." Andrea paints a picture of a broken man, consumed by a grief that seems too immense for one soul to bear. "He swore to me that he didn't do what they said he did. He'd never hurt Ashley, and I believe him."

Again, Hannah glances at Gabriel, but he won't look her way.

"Did he claim someone else killed her?" Hannah probes, her

mind dissecting every word, searching for the slip, the lie, the delusion.

"No." Andrea leans in closer, her voice dropping to a whisper. "He said something possessed him and made him do those things."

Hannah leans back and doesn't instantly reply.

Andrea's fingers continue to tap on the table. "He said that something or someone had taken over his body. He was there but not, if that makes sense. He could see himself doing all the things. He heard himself saying horrible things to her, but he couldn't stop it from happening no matter how hard he tried. It was like something had taken over, taken control of his body."

Hannah sighs. She had discussed this with Gabriel on the drive here. Even the BTK serial killer said he'd been possessed when he killed ten people.

"Many murderers claim possession," Hannah counters, her tone clinical. "It's not unheard of."

She knows she appears cold, but she has to be. Gabriel is giving all the vibes of sympathy, and someone needs to be asked the hard questions, searching for the cold truth.

"But it wasn't Brad who killed my sister." Andrea's frustration mounts, her plea for belief almost palpable.

"Then who do you think did?" Hannah's question hangs in the air, laden with a mix of doubt and fear.

Andrea's mouth opens, like she's about to say something revealing, but then she stops herself. Her eyes blink rapidly, and she looks everywhere about the room but never directly at Hannah.

"The devil." Andrea's answer finally slips out in a hushed whisper.

The silence that follows is deafening, only the distant clatter of dishes in the kitchen breaking the spell.

Hannah's thoughts race, skepticism battling against the gnawing possibility that there is more to this than the ramblings of a grieving sister. She watches as Andrea fidgets with the dainty silver cross around her neck, her eyes continually scanning the diner, her gaze on the door as if waiting for someone to walk through.

In the dim light of the diner, the seeds of a chilling truth begin to take root.

The way Andrea's hands twisted the tiny silver cross hanging around her neck is more than nerves. That cross is a talisman against unseen threats. The diner's neon light flickers, casting moving shadows over Andrea's gaunt features.

"Does your family agree with you?" Hannah asks, her voice low, almost drowned out by the hiss of the coffee machine in the background.

Andrea's head shakes, just once, the movement decisive. "My parents won't talk to me anymore." Her eyes dart to the door again.

The faded tan line on Andrea's ring finger catches Hannah's attention. "And your partner?"

Andrea glances down, her fingers brushing the pale skin where a symbol of commitment once rested. "He left me a few months ago." A heavy sigh escapes her. "I don't blame any of them. I know I sound crazy, but I swear I'm not. I've wrestled with it for months, between visiting Brad and reading scripture."

Hannah stays quiet, letting the silence between them grow, giving space for the truth be make itself known. It always does when there's silence.

"I kept visiting Brad, but he never wavered," Andrea continues, pulling at the cross as if it can confirm her words. "His story wasn't always exact, not word for word, like he'd practiced it either. Every time he'd reveal something more, some emotion he'd kept to himself, a thought or action with more detail than previously stated. Then, he showed me a drawing. Said it was who made him do it."

"Who he believes made him do it," Gabriel finally speaks up, correcting Andrea. He leans forward with keen interest. "Do you have it?"

She shakes her head, strands of hair sticking to her damp forehead. "It's with Brad in the prison."

"Right." Gabriel glances at Hannah before turning back to Andrea. "Thank you for meeting us. I know it was hard. We'll need to talk it over, do some more research on our end, and we'll be in touch, okay?"

While Gabriel takes control of the conversation, Hannah watches, taking it all in. There's more happening here than what's being said.

Andrea reaches out, her grip on Hannah's hand is surprisingly strong. "Do you believe me?"

"Yes, I believe that you believe," Hannah says carefully and thoughtfully, with a softness not meant to invoke pain. She pulls her hand away.

"But you don't believe Brad's story?" Andrea looks like she's about to cry.

"I'm not sure. Not yet."

"Andrea," Gabriel interrupts, pulling the attention toward him, "do you think you could you get us on Brad's visitor list?"

Hannah shoots him a hard look. Never once in their discussions did visiting a prison every come up.

Andrea nods, weary but determined. "I've already spoken to him about it."

"I'm sorry?" Hannah isn't sure she heard Andrea correctly.

"Well, the system is very slow and can take up to three weeks before they process any visitor requests, so after meeting with Gabriel the first time, I projected that you would come. During one of my visits to Brad, I mentioned it to him, and he put in the paperwork." She pauses as if noting the look on Hannah's face for the first time. "I just didn't want you to waste your time coming down here. That was all."

Hannah scoots out of the booth, grabs her purse, and leaves some money on the table to cover their coffees. She waits for Gabriel to join her outside.

"I don't know," she says, giving him a shrug. "I don't know what to believe, to be honest."

A fog descends like a shroud over the town, wrapping around the streetlights and obscuring the diner's neon sign.

"Come on. Let's go before it gets any worse," she tells him.

"I remember passing a hotel just up ahead. Maybe we should stay the night? It's too crazy to drive back in this." His breath is visible in the air before he opens his door and gets in.

Hannah says nothing, her eyes scanning the fog as if expecting shadows to move.

They make it only a few miles down the road, but it takes way too long, and she doesn't want to spend another minute on the road if she doesn't have to. They have the radio on, but there's no word about the fog lifting.

They pull into the hotel parking lot, and the lobby is full of other travelers like themselves, wanting a room.

"It's my last room," the woman at the counter says, glancing behind Hannah. "Hopefully, you're the last one needing it. That fog out there is something else, isn't it? Heard there's a huge five-car pileup about seven clicks down the road, so it's a good thing you stopped now."

"Good thing." Hannah's response is curt, her mind elsewhere.

Gabe offers a smile that doesn't quite reach his eyes. "Whatever you have will be fine."

They make their way to a small room with a queen bed.

"About Brad—" Gabe begins, sitting on the edge of the mattress.

"Making promises without me?" Hannah interrupts, crossing her arms. She dares him to make an excuse, to come up with something she'll believe. Why bring her here and want her opinion if the decision has already been made?

"I just..." He stops, and a haunted look crosses his features.

"Know what it's like to be possessed?" She cuts him off, a flash of anger in her eyes. She hates herself in this moment, she should be sympathetic, but he hurt her too many times, and anger is all she feels in this moment.

He nods solemnly. "It can happen."

"And let me guess. You'll know by looking at him, right? Because you know you're not allowed to touch him. Maybe things are different in the UK, but here, physical contact between inmates and visitors is strictly prohibited."

"Maybe." He shrugs, ignoring her tone. "The drawing matters."

"It could be a self-portrait." Her scoff fills the silence.

"Why do you resist the possibility?" Gabe presses, his voice low.

"Because it's usually bullshit." Her reply is sharp and punctuated by frustration. "Because thousands of men who've murdered their partners, girlfriends, wives, or women they just met all claim the same thing. 'It wasn't me. Something came over me.' It's all bullshit, and you know it." She paces the room, finger jabbing the air as she tries to get him to understand.

"True. I hear you. I do, Hannah." Gabriel lowers his voice, coming across as both calm and condescending.

Of course he would. He's a man who doesn't get it, but this is something women live with regularly.

"Fuck you," she mutters, unsure if he hears her or not. She doesn't care if he does to be honest.

"I also happen to agree whether you believe me or not." Gabriel looks at her. "But if it's not? What if, this time, it's true? Shouldn't we at least take the opportunity to find out?"

She shakes her head. He hasn't heard her at all.

"We're not the police, Gabriel. We are unable and ill-equipped to handle solving a murder case, and you know that. Please tell me this isn't for some gimmick where you tell people you've helped solve a murder due to your psychic abilities?"

Even as she says the words, guilt eats her inside, and from the look on his face, she's hurt him to the core.

She won't take them back, though. He did this after Ghost Lake by writing that book, a book he didn't even tell her about until after he sold it.

Should she apologize? No. He needs to answer the questions because they're legitimate ones.

"I deserve that, and you deserve an answer. Is there a part of me that hopes this reflects back on us with a positive spin? Sure.

The same could be said for you, too, though, right? You need another win under your belt if you're going to make this a real gig." He gets up and twists off the cap from a water bottle. "But, all that aside, Hannah, let's look at him as a person, not as a monster. What if he was possessed? What if that spirit is there, waiting for its next victim?" Gabriel's eyes are earnest and intense.

Hannah turns away, staring out the window where the fog seems to press against the glass, whispering secrets only it knows.

"We could be the ones that stop that from happening. We— you, me, the kid—could be saving a person's life, all by going to the prison and hearing the man out. That's worth it, don't you think?"

CHAPTER
EIGHT

GABRIEL

The computer screen flickers, casting an eerie glow across Riley's face, his features stark and shadowed. His wide eyes, slightly glassy, reflect the glow of his computer screen, which flickers every so often as if something in the room beyond is moving, unsettled.

"Turn on some lights, Riley," Hannah mutters. She takes a sip of her coffee. "Open a window or two, will you? The place probably needs to be aired out."

Riley nods and glances around before disappearing from the screen. A moment later, light floods the frame, revealing the messy state of the small study behind him. Stacks of books, a pizza box, to-go cups, and bits of trash clutter the space, casting chaotic shadows against the walls.

"Holy shit, kid. We haven't been gone *that* long," Gabriel remarks, shaking his head. "Could you try cleaning up?"

Riley pops back into view, giving Gabriel the finger with a half-smirk. "Real funny, you guys, but listen. I actually found something, and it's… creepy."

His voice holds a mix of excitement and unease, and Hannah

and Gabriel lean closer, staring at the screen. The steam from Hannah's coffee swirls in the air, fogging the camera momentarily. Gabriel's eyes linger on the dark circles under her eyes, and a pang of worry gnaws at him. She's been on edge, drinking coffee like water, barely sleeping. They all are.

"Show us what you found," he commands, his tone firm despite the slight tremor in his hands.

Riley's screen flickers, revealing digitized scans of faded photographs, sepia-toned images, and aged, yellowing newspaper clippings. "Look at this," Riley murmurs, scrolling slowly through each piece of evidence. "A lot of deaths all within the walls of that hotel. It's like the place is a magnet for tragedy."

Hannah's eyes darken as she studies the images. She rubs her arms, chilled, while her gaze is fixed on one particularly grim headline: *Young Woman Found Dead in Hotel Room, 1957.* The grainy black-and-white photograph of the hotel looks no different than it does now—unchanged, like it's trapped in time, unable to shake its grim legacy.

"Jesus," she murmurs, her voice barely above a whisper. "How many deaths are we talking here?"

"Twenty," Riley replies, his voice tight with suppressed tension. "That's just what I could find documented over the last ninety years."

"Twenty people." Gabriel sounds distant, almost hollow, even to himself. He can't help but feel the weight of that number, like each soul adds another layer of darkness that clings to him, to all of them. "Why didn't we see this sooner?"

Hannah's lips press together in a hard line. "So much for just another haunted hotel. This place tops every other site we've investigated. If even half of this is true… it's a damn house of horrors."

A tense silence follows, each of them digesting the implications. The hotel isn't just haunted. It is haunted by something far darker than ghost stories.

"Did you… did you talk to her?" Riley's question comes softly, almost hesitantly.

Gabriel flicks his gaze to Hannah who gives him a brief nod, her expression tense. "Yeah. Briefly. She didn't say much, but she gave us a lead on where to go next."

Riley raises an eyebrow, looking intrigued. "Where's that?"

"Brad," Gabriel replies, his tone steady but his fingers tightening around his phone. "We're going to see him in prison."

Riley's eyes widen. "No way. A prison can't be much different than the asylum, right? I mean, with all that negative energy and... shit, Gabriel, how do you handle being amidst all that?"

"It won't be easy, for sure, but what choice do we have?" The words are heavy on Gabriel's tongue. He shudders, the memories of Ghost Lake still fresh in his mind, lingering like cobwebs in his thoughts.

He looks over at Hannah. He knows the asylum's aftermath still haunts her. She's keeping it buried, but he can see it in her restless eyes. They've all been shaken—Riley included—which makes him wonder why they're so eager to risk it again.

But he knows the answer. They have to see this through.

"Just... be careful, okay?" Riley's voice cracks slightly, and his eyes dart to something offscreen. There's a fleeting look of apprehension in his gaze before he signs off.

Seconds after the call ends, Gabriel's phone buzzes, an onslaught of messages from Riley lighting up the screen. He glances over, intrigued, and Hannah leans in as they scroll through the photos together. A face stares back at them—Reginald Hopkins, an old photo from the hotel's early days. His face is grotesque—a bulbous nose, one eye smaller than the other, and a scar splitting his upper lip, giving his expression a sinister twist.

"That face," Hannah whispers, her voice hollow. "It'll haunt me till the end of time."

Gabe suppresses a shiver, but he can't shake the feeling that Hopkins, or someone like him, has left a twisted mark on the hotel. Maybe his presence lingers, clinging to the walls, an indelible stain on a place already soaked with misery.

The tension tightens as Gabriel's phone rings, Andrea's name flashing across the screen. He answers, listening as she delivers the news in clipped, efficient sentences: they've been granted a slot to see Brad in person. If they hustle, they can make it to the prison by early afternoon.

"If we leave now," Gabriel says, glancing at the time, "we've got just enough time to grab some real food and coffee before we go." He grabs the keys and tosses Hannah's purse to her.

She opens her mouth to object.

He cuts her off with a determined look that says *this is happening*. "Come on," he urges, not giving her any room for doubt.

The entire drive, the weight of their destination hangs heavy between them. Gabriel's fingers grip the steering wheel a bit too tightly, and Hannah, in the passenger seat, keeps stealing glances out the window, her face pale with whatever she's trying to keep hidden.

The silence is thick and charged, and neither of them dares to break it as they approach the prison. Each mile brings them closer to a place steeped in darkness, another layer of shadows they're choosing to walk into. The air in the car feels tense and claustrophobic, as if the closer they get, the more tightly the specters of their last investigation close in on them.

Finally, as the gray prison looms into view, towering and stark, Hannah takes a shaky breath. "You ready for this?"

Gabriel glances over. "Not at all," he admits, forcing a slight smile. "But we're doing it anyway."

They step out of the car, and the chill of the prison's shadow settles over them. For a second, Gabriel's hand brushes hers, and the small contact feels like an anchor in the storm of dread rising in his chest. They exchange a glance, a silent, unspoken understanding between them. They're in this together, come what may.

Soon, they would find themselves face to face with Brad, a man who may hold the key to the hotel's dark secrets... or the doorway to a darkness far greater than any of them could imagine.

CHAPTER
NINE

The prison looms ahead like a fortress built to repel both escape and hope.

Against the stark midday sky, its gray walls reach endlessly, imposing and cold, a hulking relic of despair. While Hannah leads, Gabriel follows behind her, walking down a narrow, sterile corridor, their footsteps echoing off the unforgiving concrete floors.

The air smells faintly metallic, tinged with disinfectant and something heavier, something that feels ancient and oppressive, like years of unresolved suffering embedded in the walls. A distant door clangs shut, the sound reverberating down the hall, each metallic echo trailing behind them like the shadows of lost souls.

A guard with a face as expressionless as stone stops them in their tracks, informing them curtly that their visit with Brad isn't guaranteed.

"So we drove all this way for nothing?" Gabriel mutters under his breath, the frustration starting to gnaw at him.

"Knock it off," Hannah hisses, her tone cutting through the cold air like a blade. Her gaze is fixed forward, unblinking, her face drawn and pale under the harsh fluorescent lights. She looks just as tired as he feels, maybe more.

The wait stretches endlessly, each tick of the clock a maddening reminder of time slipping by, fraying Gabriel's nerves further. The sterile walls, the faint hum of the overhead lights, the oppressive silence—everything here seems designed to break people down.

When a guard finally gestures for them to follow, Gabriel nearly exhales in relief, but the sound catches in his throat as he surrenders his belongings, the finality of the moment settling heavy in his chest.

They pass through a series of locked doors, each one sliding closed with a resounding thud, trapping them deeper within the belly of the prison. Gabriel's stomach churns, a dull ache twisting as he feels the walls closing in.

The guard finally leads them to "Number 7," a row of booths divided by scratched plexiglass barriers. The space is cavernous, its high ceilings swallowing sounds and bouncing back only echoes—an eerie symphony of whispers, shuffling footsteps, and muffled conversations.

Gabriel takes a seat in one of the hard, plastic chairs, the unyielding surface offering no comfort, amplifying the discomfort already brewing inside him. Hannah's hand finds his shoulder, squeezing lightly as she sits beside him.

He knows she can feel the tension radiating from him, but she doesn't say anything, just offers her quiet support, grounding him. She has no idea how much he dreads places like this. Even with her there, a chill runs through him.

Moments later, Brad shuffles into view on the other side of the plexiglass, his wrists shackled, flanked by two guards. His eyes dart around, wide and unfocused, brimming with a mixture of fear and confusion. He looks like a man haunted, not just by what he's done, but by something far darker, something intangible yet all-consuming.

He takes his seat, the barrier between them cold and imper- sonal, and leans forward, his voice barely above a whisper.

"Andrea said you might be able to help me," he says, his voice cracked, raw, as if it's been unused for a long time.

Hannah's eyes narrow slightly. Her voice is barely audible as she replies, "We're not miracle workers."

Brad looks down, his shoulders slumping further, resignation etched into his very posture. Gabriel watches him closely, trying to read the man's expression, searching for any sign of deception or delusion.

"Tell me about that night," Gabriel says, fixing Brad with an unrelenting stare. He suppresses a shiver as goosebumps prickle over his arms, as though the darkness Brad encountered has somehow reached across the plexiglass, touching him, cold and insidious.

"Anything strange, anything out of the ordinary?" Hannah asks. "How was Ashley? Did she seem... different in any way?"

Brad's gaze flickers as he searches for the right words. "It was... just a regular night," he says slowly, his voice strained, as if he's struggling to hold onto the memory. "We were excited to be there. It was a nice hotel that offered a great sweetheart package, complete with the honeymoon suite, dinner, and wine. Old, sure, and a little rundown, but the price was good, and the restaurant came highly recommended." He pauses, his brow furrowing, his gaze unfocused. "But then... there were the whispers."

Gabriel exchanges a quick, tense glance with Hannah, his pulse quickening. "Whispers?" he prompts, leaning closer.

"Yeah," Brad continues, his eyes going distant, like he's peering into a memory he'd rather forget. "It sounded like someone was in the room with us, like voices were coming through the vents or something. They were faint, just at the edge of hearing, and sometimes I thought they were in the corner, just out of sight." He lets out a shaky breath. "Ashley thought it was just mice in the walls... but it didn't feel right."

Gabriel's skin prickles, the familiar, icy grip of unease settling over him. "And... the pain?" he asks, his voice barely steady. He can already feel his own head throbbing, a phantom echo of whatever Brad might have felt that night.

Brad's face twists, his eyes clouding with fear. "It was like... something was inside my head, pushing against my skull, digging its fingers into my brain. I took a bunch of painkillers, but it didn't help. It got worse, like needles stabbing my brain, over and over."

The room feels colder, the light harsher, as Gabriel listens, his hand tightening around the edge of the table. "What else?" he asks, forcing himself to maintain his composure despite the growing unease clawing at his insides.

Brad's voice drops, almost a whisper. "I blacked out. When I came to... I was on top of Ashley, stabbing her. I could see my hand moving, feel the blade cutting into her skin, but it was like... I wasn't in control. I tried to stop, but it was like something else was holding my arm, forcing me." His voice cracks, and he looks down at his trembling hands.

"Afterward, I found bruises on my wrist—finger marks, like something had gripped me," he continues. "They told me it was probably Ashley, that she was fighting me off, but..." He trails off, his face crumpling. "I don't think it was her."

Gabriel swallows, his throat dry, the image Brad paints vivid and chilling. He knows Hannah feels it too; her expression is taut, her eyes locked on Brad, absorbing every fractured word. They'd agreed not to let Brad see any hint of belief, to remain objective, but it's hard—harder than he anticipated.

"Andrea mentioned a drawing," Gabriel says, seizing the lifeline of facts, trying to bring the conversation back to something tangible. "Can we see it?"

Brad hesitates, then reaches into his pocket, fumbling with a folded piece of paper. His hands tremble as he presses it against the plexiglass.

The sketch is frantic, raw, the lines jagged and heavy as though he'd etched it from a place of desperation. Amidst the chaotic scribbles, a face stares back at them—grotesque, a caricature of malice with a bulbous nose, one eye larger than the other, and a deep scar splitting his mouth.

Gabriel feels a chill seep into his bones as he stares at the figure. "It's him," he murmurs, barely audible, his voice laced with grim certainty. "Reginald Hopkins. Or... his spirit, at least."

Hannah's eyes are wide, and she gives a barely perceptible nod. She sees it too.

Brad's gaze is fixed on the drawing, his face pale, his expression haunted. He's lost somewhere between memory and nightmare, the line between them blurred beyond recognition. He finally looks up, his eyes meeting Gabriel's, filled with a desperate, unspoken plea.

"Please," he whispers, his voice trembling. "Tell me I didn't do this... not of my own will."

Gabriel glances at Hannah, his chest tightening. The answer teeters on the edge of his mind, tangled with the impossible horror of the truth. "We'll find out," he says, his voice steady, even as the weight of that promise settles over him like a shadow. "But whatever's haunting that hotel, it's not done yet."

CHAPTER
TEN

HANNAH

Hannah's fingers tremble slightly as she reaches for her phone. With a swift tap, the screen illuminates, revealing the gallery where an old, grainy photo of Reginald Hopkins. The lines and contours of the face in the drawing dance into place alongside the man's features in the photograph. Beside her, Gabriel stiffens.

She enlarges the image and holds it against the Plexiglas that separates them from Brad. "Look at this," she says, her voice calm, almost reverent.

Bran leans in, his breath fogging a small circle on the glass. "That's him," he says, his finger jabbing at the paper he's still holding up. "The man I keep seeing. It's him."

"When do you see him?" Gabriel asks.

"When don't I? The second I close my eyes, I see his face, not hers, not Ashley's. When I walk to my cell, it's like he's beside me." Brad's eyes, wide with fear and hope, met theirs through the barrier. "Please, you have to help me or at least find out the truth about the hotel so no one else has to die."

"Time's up," a gruff voice sounds, and behind them, a guard appears.

Hannah and Gabriel push back their chairs and turn away, neither promising their help nor indicating the lack thereof.

Outside, the chill air bites at their exposed skin. Hannah wraps her arms around herself, not just for warmth but for comfort.

She breaks the silence, her voice cutting through the cold. "Did you get what you needed? You know we're only giving him false hope. Even if we prove there's a ghost in that hotel possessing people, that won't exonerate him. He still did it, possessed or not. No court is ever going to have ghost haunting as a defense."

"Maybe, maybe not, but instead of thinking we can clear his name, maybe we can get him moved to a treatment facility instead," Gabriel suggests, his eyes searching hers for approval.

She doesn't answer, not because she doesn't want to but because she doesn't need to. She's said her piece, and so has Gabriel.

The journey to the airport is muted, the task ahead pressing into Hannah's thoughts. It's more than dealing with angry and restless spirits. It's battling unseen forces that can and have harmed others. That thought alone scares the shit out of her. She thought Gabriel had died at Ghost Asylum. What if next time it's her or Riley?

"Are we doing this?" Gabe asks quietly.

"I'll be honest. I don't know if I want to take it on. It's so complicated, and it's not just about putting the spirits to rest or cleansing the place, is it?"

"But if doing so can stop that spirit from hurting others, don't you agree it's worth the risk?" Gabriel asks the question she's been trying to avoid.

After a moment's hesitation, Hannah nods. "You're right. We'll check for hauntings, but first, we need Riley. We can't do this without him and his equipment."

Hannah texts Riley to start packing up and that they were on their way back. Their flight from San Diego to Vancouver wasn't very long and the whole flight home, Hannah made a list of all the things they needed to bring and the things they needed to do once they returned to San Diego.

Riley picks them up at the airport, his enthusiasm palpable the whole ride back to the cottage and while as he packs up all the necessary equipment. While Riley handles that, she books plane tickets and asks Gabriel to check the hotel website for rooms.

"We should probably try to stay on the twelfth or fourteenth floor, right?" Gabriel mentions. "To do that, we'll need to call."

She sends him the phone number. "Go for it."

While he calls the hotel, Hannah heads to the backyard and opens the small gate leading to the beach. A walk by the shore, digging her toes into the sand and listening to the seagulls, is what she needs right now. Things are about to get chaotic and messy, and she needs to be in the right frame of mind.

Sure enough, two hours later, she's back at the rental, her steps lighter, her heart easy, and she's ready to do what it takes to ensure no one gets hurt.

At the airport, security halts Riley, his gear drawing suspicion. Hannah steps up, trying to offer a reasonable explanation without diving into the unbelievable truth of their profession, but Riley blurts it out, earning chuckles from the guards. They are waved through with a shake of heads and smirking in disbelief.

In their cramped economy seats, Riley casts curious glances at Hannah and Gabriel. "Is something wrong?" he finally asks, leaning closer to Hannah.

She exhales slowly. She wants to say no, but then that might make Riley feel like a child caught between two bickering parents. "Just different opinions on this case."

"So what, like, no arguments or anything? I thought you two were fighting or something," Riley prods, oblivious to the tension he's stirring.

Hannah glances over toward Gabriel, but he's got his earphones in and isn't paying them any attention. "Fighting? What do you mean?"

"Like you know, arguments that couples sometimes have… That kind of fighting. Just make up, will you?"

She gives a short snort. "No. And we are not a couple, for your information. There's just a difference of opinions when it comes to this case. That's all." Hannah's tone is sharper than she intended.

The look on Riley's face tells her he doesn't believe her. "So why are we doing it then if you don't agree?"

Hannah shrugs. "Because I realize I'm reacting based on the fear of the unknown, and if anyone is going to do this, it might as well be us."

"Riiiigght," Riley says, clearly not believing her. "Whatever you say."

Riley retreats into his own world, earbuds in place, leaving Hannah to stare at the seatback in front of her, lost in thought about what horrors might lurk within the hotel's walls.

When they arrive, it's in the middle of a clusterfuck of tension and aggravation. The vehicle she rented wasn't available, and they had almost been stuck in a tiny little Hyundai Kona before Gabriel turned on his charm and sweet-talked the girl behind the desk to upgrading them to a larger SUV. Then, they got lost on the drive, the map on her phone updating in the middle of their trip. Needless to say, Hannah's nerves are shot, and she could do with a nice glass of wine and a moment of reprieve from the two males.

Except that's not going to happen. They're here to work.

The hotel's grand lobby looms ahead, its opulence marred by an undercurrent of something sinister. Hannah hesitates at the threshold, a shiver coursing through her despite the warmth.

Gabriel's hand casually brushes against hers. She glances up to catch the shadow of unease on his face.

"Feel that?" she murmurs.

"Like walking into a cold spot," he replies, his voice low.

They approach the front desk. They'd booked two rooms, and one gets upgraded, the honeymoon suite on the twelfth floor. Which, coincidentally, is the same room Brad and Ashley stayed in. They'd tried to request it previously, but it had been booked up.

"I'd like the room directly above that one, on the upper floor, if it's available," Gabriel says.

"Above it? Sure, let me look…" Her fingers tap dance over the keyboard, but when she looks up, it's with a bit of a frown. "Well, the room directly above the honeymoon suite is a junior suite, but it's in the older part of the wing and hasn't been updated yet."

"That's fine. We'll take it."

"I can give you a much nicer room on the other end," she says.

"Nope. That one will be perfect."

When the clerk glances at Hannah, Hannah just offers her a tight smile and a slight shrug.

"Here are your keys," the girl says, handing over an actual key with a red room tag attached. "Mr. Locke will assist you with your bags." The clerk nods toward the concierge approaching them.

Mr. Locke is an older man in his mid-fifties, tall and reedy, with thinning hair that he combs over and a twisted smile revealing crooked and stained teeth. "My desk is available at all times," he tells them, offering a luggage cart for all their equipment. "If I'm not on shift, my colleague will be." He offers them a card with a too-practiced grin.

"Thank you." Hannah pockets the card without giving it too much attention. Her gaze is focused on a sign.

"Ghost tours," Gabriel mutters as they head toward the elevator, nodding at the sign. "Cashing in on the hauntings."

"We should sign up for a tour," Riley piques up. "That would be cool and might give us some insider information on this place."

"Sure, kid. You go for it," Gabriel tells him.

Once inside the elevator, their luggage and the luggage cart filling up most of the space, Gabriel's fingers hovering over the buttons. "I still don't like this," he says, frowning slightly. "We shouldn't be splitting up."

"We've already been over this," she reminds him. "It's the best way to investigate both floors surrounding the thirteen one that is off limits. I'll be fine if that's what you're worried about."

"You're in the same room Brad and Ashley were," he presses. Concern for her safety is all over him.

Hannah gives his hand a slight squeeze. "I will be fine," she reminds him. "I'm alone, and as far as we know, our spirit is only attracted to couples." Hannah's voice wavers slightly as she tries to reassure him. "So, um, maybe make it very obvious that you two aren't a couple?" She wiggles her brows, her laughter forced.

Riley grimaces.

Gabriel snorts. "More like combative father and son," he mutters beneath his breath.

"Hey, I never asked you to take on that role, big guy. We're colleagues, nothing more." Riley shakes his head before tilting his gaze upward to watch the numbers light up.

The elevator dings open, and when Hannah steps onto the twelfth floor, nausea hits hard. She clutches her stomach, bile rising.

"There's a lot of bad energy here. I don't like it." Gabriel's lips tighten as he steps out behind her. "Come on, kid. I want to check out her room before we head to ours."

Riley looks at all the luggage with a questioning glance. "Um, you gonna help me then?"

Hannah struggles to not roll her eyes as she grabs hold of the luggage rack and pulls it forward.

No one says anything once they're inside her room. The honeymoon suite isn't anything too special, there's a king size bed, a dresser with a television, a nightstand with a lamp and phone, and a door to the bathroom. No ghosts are jumping out, and there are no defining cold zones as she walks about the room. There is an oppressiveness, but it's not overwhelming, just like a gentle brush reminding them that something is wrong.

Hannah unpacks her suitcase while Riley lays out the new equipment: an EMF reader, thermometer, and infrared goggles.

Hannah's phone rings. She glances down at the screen with surprise. "Um, you guys finish setting up, I'll take this out in the hall. It's my mom."

"Are you sure?" Gabriel hesitates as he opens the door for her. "Don't go too far, okay?"

"I'll be fine." She waves off his concern, not sure how to react to him right now. She steps out and answers the call. "Hey, Mom. What's up? Is everything okay?"

Instead of her mom's voice, she hears crackling static.

"Mom? Are you there?" Her voice rises over the noise. It reminds her of the white noise of a fuzzy television station.

"...danger..." A woman's voice briefly breaks through. "...leave..." More static. "...you will die..."

The call ends abruptly with an alarm blaring. Hannah pulls the phone away from her ear, her heart racing as the alarm continues for another three seconds before it stops.

Hannah looks at the now blank screen on her phone. What the hell was that?

She pulls up her mother's number and calls her. "Hey, Mom. Quick question, but um, did you just call me?"

"Oh, yes, but I hung up because it was such a bad connection, I figured you couldn't hear me." Her mother's tone was a little dismissive. "I just wanted to remind you that your father's birthday is coming up and we were thinking of heading to Vancouver Island, in case you were thinking of coming and surprising him."

"So... you were just calling me to tell me not to come home for Dad's birthday. Got it." She doesn't say that she forgot all about his birthday coming up and that she had no plans to return home anyway.

"Right. If you're around, though, why don't you take the ferry over to the island for a day and join us for dinner one night? A friend of ours is lending us their cabin for a week."

After making some casual plans, Hannah hangs up and heads back into the room where Gabriel and Riley are waiting. She tells them about the static and the haunting words and finishes with, "I think we just had our first contact."

CHAPTER
ELEVEN

GABRIEL

Gabriel and Riley leave Hannah's room and repack the elevator with all their luggage. Riley hesitates before pressing the button for the fourteenth floor, Hannah's words ringing in his ears.

"Do you think it's true?" Riley asks.

"What's true? The phone call?" Gabriel looks at the kid for the longest time and realizes he's trying to mask his fear and put on a brave front. "I think, no matter what we do or where we go, as long as we are trying to free the spirits from these hauntings, they're always going to fight us."

"So, we're always going to live with our lives in danger?"

Gabriel shrugs. The idea doesn't bother him. "The threat to our lives will always be there, sure, but come on. We're a bloody good team who knows how to crack some spiritual skulls, don't you think?" He tries to add some brevity to his voice, but it falls flat.

The elevator creaks up to the next floor, groaning and shuddering.

"I guess," Riley says. "I don't like leaving Hannah alone, though. I'm with you on that."

"Well, like she said, she's there alone and our spirit seems more inclined to attack couples."

Does he believe that? Hell no, but for the kid's sake, he'll pretend he does.

As they slowly ascend to their floor, a chilling wind slithers around their ankles, causing Gabriel's fingers to clench tightly at his side before he reaches out to place them, palms flat, on the elevator door.

"Um, what are you doing?"

"Did you sense that?" Gabriel squints suspiciously.

"Sense what?" Riley looks at him.

"A chill. Right here." He taps the metal door. "As if we crossed through a cold spot."

"The ghost of the thirteenth floor making its presence known?" Riley attempts a joke, but unease tinges his voice.

"I wonder if maybe there's a hidden passage," Gabriel muses aloud, stroking his chin thoughtfully. "An old service staircase or something."

"Possibly. We could cross-check with the original blueprints at city hall," Riley suggests. "They should have something from when it was first constructed in their archives."

With a ding, the doors part to reveal a corridor cloaked in faded peeling wallpaper and lights flickering ominously. They enter the dimly lit hallway, where shadows dance eerily on the walls.

"Dude, if this doesn't give off freaky ghost vibes, I don't know what does." Riley's voice sounds loud in the narrow space.

Suddenly, three figures emerge around the corner—two men and a woman, all about Riley's age. The woman locks eyes with Riley, a subtle smile playing on her lips.

Cleary caught off guard by her stare, Riley stumbles mid-step and collides with the wall. His bag hits the ground, and zippers bursting open, and an EMF reader skidding across the floor.

"Fuuuucckk," Riley mutters as he quickly bends to retrieve his things.

"Whoa there!" One of the guys picks up the device curiously.

"Is this an EMF reader? No shit, it is! You guys hunting ghosts too?"

Gabriel snatches it from the guy and puts it in one of the bags. "Not as fancy as that. Just exploring," he replies sharply.

"Well, you should, especially with that shit you've got. We've got some of the same stuff back in our rooms. We're here to find some ghosts." He winks. "We're known as the Phantom Phinders," he boasts. "Ring any bells?"

Gabriel cocks his head and gives the guy an "are you serious look." "Sorry, mate, can't say it does," he says, his tone British dry.

"No? Well, you should look us up. We've got over 20K followers on our YouTube channel. I'm Zach. This is Sienna, and that other shithead is Isaac." He points to the others next to him. "We're here for Murder Hotel's maid ghost tale. Heard she poisoned someone and now roams these halls."

"Murder Hotel?" Gabriel tries not to laugh.

"Yeah, it's all the rage and what the hashtags are, man. You should check it out."

"Cool. Thanks for letting us know," Riley interjects while hoisting the repacked bags over his shoulder. "Watch out for those phantoms!" he calls out as they walk away.

Sienna gives Riley a little wave and then puckers her lips into a kiss before the trio chuckles among themselves as they vanish into shadows that seem to swallow them whole.

"Amateurs," Gabriel mutters as they continue down the hallway toward their room.

"They're actually pretty good. I follow them," Riley says a little sheepishly, looking down the hall again.

"Of course you do," Gabriel mumbles as he pulls out his old-fashioned key and inserts it into the door. "You'd think they'd update their locks to keyless entry."

"I think it goes with the whole vibe, don't you?" Riley pushes open the door, enters the room, and drops the bags with a thud in the middle of the room. "That group might come in handy, though," he suggests.

Gabriel clocked the way Riley focused on the girl and shakes his head. The kid could get them in trouble if they're not careful.

Gabriel glances around, noticing the dust motes dancing in the light from the crack in the curtains. The room is dimly lit, with only a small window in the corner partially closed by a threadbare curtain. The walls are painted a dull, faded blue, and the floor is made of worn, creaky wooden boards covered in old carpet. A musty smell hangs in the air, mixed with a hint of lavender from an old candle on the windowsill. The furniture is mismatched and worn, with threadbare cushions and chipped paint.

This room has not been used or cared for in quite some time, which explains why the reservation desk was very hesitant about giving him a room above Hannah's.

"Don't get distracted," Gabriel warns him. "We're not here to mix business with pleasure, young Riley. Keep it in your pants."

"Haha! Coming from you? London's elusive heartbreaker," Riley teases playfully despite the oppressive atmosphere enveloping them like a heavy cloak of dread. "Mate, I don't like this room. There's something about it."

"Hopefully, we won't be here long. We should be right above Hannah's, so whatever you're feeling, she probably is too."

Gabriel pulls out his phone and sends her a quick text. *I'm going to stomp on the floor. Tell me if you hear me.*

He does three quick bangs with the heel of his foot.

You're two floors above me, so no, but I can hear you two through the vents, Mr. Heartbreaker.

Well, shit.

"Hannah can hear us," Gabriel says, lowering his voice, "and I was far from London's heartbreaker."

Riley snorts. "Yeah, right. I looked you up. There's a shit ton of articles online about your scorned lovers. There's even a Reddit thread."

Gabriel groans. That blasted Reddit thread will be the death of him.

"All speculation." Gabriel waves a hand dismissively and

opens a case of sensors that glint malevolently under the flickering lights.

"I don't know. I kind of believe it, you know? Like, you're how old and you've never settled down? You're not big on commitment, are you?" Riley prods gently although his focus is fixated on the blinking equipment lights.

"With the schedule I kept, settling down was never really a thing," Gabriel grumbles.

"And what about recently?"

Gabriel knows precisely what Riley is alluding to. "I was on a book tour."

"Sure." Riley gives him a look that says more than it should. "Whatever makes you feel better about abandoning Hannah." He turns his back on Gabriel to unpack more equipment.

CHAPTER
TWELVE

HANNAH

The grand lobby is a cavernous space, shadows clinging to the ornate corners where light fears to tread. Their footsteps clatter off the cracked marble floors as they approach each other beneath the looming chandelier.

Once upon a time, this place would have been opulent and luxurious. Now, even with the old world touches, it carries a feeling of worn tiredness aged with neglect.

"I just can't get over the fact there are actual ghost hunters at this hotel at the same time as us." Riley nudges her arm. "I mean, what are the coincidences?"

"Considering they host ghost tours regularly, I'd be surprised if there weren't more ghost hunters here." Hannah looks around and almost misses the way the smile on Riley's face falters. "But to have a group that's so popular, I think it's cool."

At breakfast, he wouldn't stop talking about the Phantom Phinders. He made them watch video after video like he was trying to prove something.

"Riley thinks we can use that group," Gabriel says.

Ah, that's it, then.

"They could prove to be useful," Hannah says, knowing this is what Riley's hoping she would say. To be honest, her mind is still on the static-filled call from last night. "As long as there's no risk to our work and why we're here." She gives him a stern look. "We're not here for the thrills and views."

Gabriel clears his throat. "But they also wouldn't hurt. Maybe that's something we should consider..."

"What? Are you kidding me right now?" Hannah is shocked he'd actually bring this up, considering everything he's been through and how he had been eviscerated by social media in the past. "No, absolutely not."

"I'm not saying I'm a fan, but if we want our work to spread and make some money..."

"We're not in this for the money," she says. Should she be surprised she has to remind him of this? "I thought we were all on the same page here."

She groans with frustration at Riley and Gabriel's shared look.

"We are. We just think it's time to add a new page, that's all."

She sighs. "Can we discuss this later?"

She's lost this round, and she knows it, but, if they're going to do it—go online—she needs to give the idea her full attention, and right now, all she's concerned about is what's happening in this building.

"So... about asking the Phantom Phinders... want me to take care of that?"

"Since Riley has the hots for the girl, I think he should be the one in charge of pumping her for information." Gabriel gives Riley a cheeky grin, which Riley returns.

Hannah rolls her eyes. "Fine. Let's see what they have to say and what they can offer."

She feels a cold draft and looks around, but she's unsure where it's coming from since all the doors appear closed.

"Listen, last night on that phone call," she says slowly, "I heard something... in the static."

"You said that. Do you think it was a warning?" Gabriel's brow furrows.

"Or just interference. I mean, considering this place and the fact they probably haven't done many renovations...the fact we get any cell signal is a bonus." She shrugs, but her gut is twisted with doubt.

"Interference due to faulty wires or from the bad energy that's here," Gabriel muses, glancing around the expansive lobby.

"Twenty murders will do that," she points out. "It's not solid proof, though."

"We still need the blueprints for the thirteenth floor," Riley reminds them.

"Do you think we can get that from the front desk? I mean, they probably get asked this all the time," Hannah suggests with a hint of skepticism.

"I still think going to City Hall might be our best bet," Riley says, "but it wouldn't hurt to ask."

At the front desk, the clerk raises an eyebrow at Hannah's request for a floor plan. "Why would you need that?"

"Research," she says, meeting a wall of suspicion.

"Listen, honey," the lady says, smacking her lips, "any research information you need on this hotel can be found online, okay?" She points to a QR code taped to the counter. "I wouldn't have taken you for ghost hunters. I need you to sign a waiver if you want to film inside our walls to post online."

"A waiver? All I want are blueprints." Hannah lets her frustration show.

Gabriel steps up, his British charm oozing. The clerk hands over a very basic map of the hotel and its amenities.

"This shows us nothing," Hannah mutters, handing over the basic map to Gabriel. "This shows nothing of the thirteenth floor, how it's blocked off, or any access points." She throws the woman a shaded look.

"What is with you?" Gabriel asks.

"The coffee here is disgusting," she mutters.

She knows she's off and sounded churlish, but she can't seem to shake it off. She barely slept last night, which probably doesn't help.

"The first thing we need to do is find a decent coffee shop

before we head to City Hall." Riley pulls up his phone. "There's one just down the road."

Once they make it to the car, Riley's excitement is palpable. "We should take our coffees down to the beach," he says. "I notice you're always in a better mood after some beach time."

"We're working, not vacationing," Hannah snaps.

"Easy, Hannah," Gabriel says, concern edging his voice. "You seem tense. Is everything okay?"

She wants to confide in him and spill her fears like scattered beads, but old wounds hold her back. He'll leave. He did last time. He will again.

"Let's just focus on the case after we get our coffee," she deflects, staring out the window, the distant waves mirroring her troubled thoughts.

After they grab coffee, it doesn't take them long to arrive at City Hall. The building itself is bright and gleaming, and after a maze of trying to find the office they need, Hannah finally stops to ask a man sitting behind one of the security desks.

He gives the three of them a look over and finally nods. "Down the hall, to your left." His eyes narrow slightly as he points toward the archives department.

"Here we go," Gabriel whispers, a half-smirk on his face as he opens the door to the archive office.

An older woman sits behind the main desk, her hair a tangle of gray curls, eyes bright like shards of glass catching the light. She perks up at the sight of Gabriel, something kindred sparking in her gaze.

"Can I help you, handsome?" Her voice is a crackling fire, warm yet unpredictable.

"Blueprints of the Brantley Hotel, please," Gabriel asks, leaning on the desk with the easy confidence that flows off of him.

"Ah! The Brantley. That's a popular one. You know what the kids nowadays call it, right? The Murder Hotel. Can you imagine?" she says, standing abruptly. "Give me a moment, and I'll be back."

Hannah can't deny the twist in her gut seeing the woman fawn over Gabriel.

Riley snickers and jabs Gabriel in the side. "Like I was saying last night. Heartbreaker. Even the old ones can't help but go all gaga over you."

"Shut it, kid." Gabriel hisses, his cheeks flaming bright red.

Hannah can feel her brows furrow as she stares at the two.

"Don't ask," Gabriel grumbles, not looking at her.

Before she can even think about how to respond, the woman returns with a tube tucked beneath her arm if she wants to. "Well, here you go," she says.

"Thank you so much." Gabriel gives her a wide smile.

"I always aim to deliver…" She gives Gabriel a wink and then eyes up Riley. "Come back in a few years, baby…"

Riley chokes back a laugh.

"Now, about the Brantley, oh, the stories that place could tell!" She opens up the tube and pulls out the papers. "There are a lot of juicy secrets from when it was built, secrets not many know about."

"Secrets?" Hannah pulls out the notebook she stashed in her purse earlier.

"The place almost didn't get built," the woman says. "If it wasn't for the secret investor…"

"Secret investor, you say?" Gabe prompts.

"Reginald Hopkins, he was quite the fellow." Her eyes sparkle as she lays out the blueprints on a light table. "Now, you want to talk about heartbreak…"

Riley has his phone out, recording the conversation. "Affairs?" he asks.

"Oh, yes," The woman looks up and pulls back. "Are you filming me, young man? I don't want to be finding myself in some sex video thanks to your use of AI or anything." She folds her arms across her chest, pushing her breasts out.

"Oh, no, ma'am. This is just for our records, in case we forget anything. Although…now that you mention it…" He casts Hannah a look. "If we do happen to use any of this for social media, would you be okay with it? Like in a documentary-type video." He swallows hard while Hannah looks on with a frown.

"Well, since you asked so nicely, you have my permission. Now…" She taps the blueprints. "Back to business. Reginald Hopkins had a lot of lovers over the years, and he liked to use that hotel as his personal love shack until he married his young wife. The poor thing. I believe her name was Darla. They lived on the thirteen floor, top floor back then. Can you imagine? Who builds a hotel with exactly thirteen floors? Except I, too, know the answer to that. Reginald Hopkins. He insisted actually."

"Really?" Gabriel leans forward.

"Oh, let me tell you. There was a lot of pushback. No one built buildings that many floors back then, but Reginald wanted to be the first. Even though he was a secret investor, he didn't hide his pride in the hotel. Money exchanged hands, and Reginald made it so that he could do whatever he wanted whenever he wanted."

"Talk about power, man. He must have been swimming in money" Riley whistles.

"Money, lovers, … anything he desired, he had," the woman confirms. "Even adding extra floors to the hotel."

"Money talks," Hannah mutters, scribbling notes.

"From the beginning of time." The woman laughs, pointing out the intricate details of the forbidden floor. "Money talks even to city planners. Now…" She points to Riley. "You'll want to take photos of these because I'm not handing out copies."

"Yes, ma'am." Riley stops videoing and takes copious amounts of photos.

The woman leans close to Hannah, her voice dropping to a conspiratorial whisper. "Darla disappeared, you know. Some say she fled with a lover, that she couldn't stand the old man she'd ended up marrying, while others…"

"Let me guess. Murder?" Gabriel adds, his eyes locked on the plans.

"Buried in the walls, or so they say," the woman says. "Another rumor is that during his marriage, Reginald was having an affair with one of the maids, who ended up poisoning him."

Hannah nods. "That one we knew about."

"Did you know that some believe the maid and Darla were in cahoots to rob Reginald and were also lovers?" She giggles behind a wrinkled hand. "Some say she killed Reginald for revenge."

"Revenge?" Hannah's hand shake slightly as she writes this down. This changed a lot.

"Or suicide." The woman shrugs, but her eyes are lit up. "There's a lot of speculation, but who knows what's the truth anymore. The dead keep their secrets."

No one says anything for a moment. Hannah glances at Riley and Gabriel and can see them digesting all they've heard.

"Well, thank you," Hannah says, closing her notepad. "This has been… illuminating."

"I'm happy to share!" the woman beams as they turn to leave. "Mind if I leave you with one more rumor?"

Gabriel stops at the door and turns back. "Absolutely," he says.

"They say one of Reginald's bastard descendants has worked in that hotel since his death. I know there's a lot of talk about ghosts and hauntings, but if you ask me, that's who you should be looking for."

CHAPTER
THIRTEEN

HANNAH

Heading back to the hotel is the last thing Hannah wants to do. She feels out of sorts and knows she's taking it out on the guys, which isn't fair to them. The coffee from earlier barely created a dent in her miserable mood, so without asking if anyone wanted a refill, she heads to a nearby cafe and points to one of the outdoor tables.

"Anyone want anything?" She lifts one eyebrow and dares either one of them to comment on her needing more coffee.

"I'll take a hot black coffee since you're offering." Gabriel takes a seat and kicks out an opposite chair for Riley.

"Same but cold, please." Riley moves the chair to give himself a little space from Gabriel.

Hannah heads inside, ignores all the other people sitting at tables, and goes directly to the counter. She places her order, pulls out her phone, and checks her messages. She needs to get out of this funk she's in.

Once the drinks are ready, she gathers all three in her hands, nudges the door open with her hip, and heads back to the table.

When she left the boys, there'd only been the two of them. Now, three others are standing between Riley and Gabriel.

One of the trio nods to Hannah as she sets the drinks on the table and takes her seat. "Hey, I'm Zach." He turns his attention to Gabriel. "I can't believe you're that old TV psychic. I checked you out last night. Gabriel Ambrose, you're quite the legend."

Gabriel raises an eyebrow, a playful glint in his eyes. "I take offense to the old part."

Hannah notices he doesn't discount the legend part. So typical.

"I have the sight too," Zach boasts, chest puffing out.

There's a stifled amusement on Gabriel's face as he manages a nod. "Really? That's... cool." He inflicts a small measure of interest in his voice, but that's about it.

"And you all found that body at Ghost Asylum, right?" Zach presses.

"Excuse us," Hannah interjects sharply. "Nice to meet you and all that, but we're in the middle of something and need to talk." She looks to the other two and figures the girl is the one Riley is gaga over.

From how she leans in, setting her hand on the back of Riley's seat, she knows it too.

"We're hosting a séance tonight. You should come." She tilts her head to look down at Riley directly and gives him a seductive smile.

Riley smiles at her like a goofy lovesick moron. "Sounds—"

"We'll pass," Hannah cuts him off. "Thanks for the offer, though."

After a few moments of awkwardness, the trio finally moves on, heading into the cafe but not before all three look at them from over their shoulders.

"That was kind of rude and very unlike you," Riley says to Hannah once the door closes. The only thing in his gaze is confusion. "Why so harsh?"

"We need to stay focused on what we came here to do and not get distracted by..." She waves dismissively toward ghost hunters who are now in the store. "...whatever they're here to do."

"Seems like we're all here for the same reasons. Maybe they'll be successful," Gabriel suggests.

"Or maybe they'll call on something they can't handle and will get hurt. Do you want that on your conscience? Because I can tell you, I don't." Hannah shoots back. "Can we please just focus on what we learned and what we'll need to do with that information before we head back to the hotel?"

"Why don't we just head there now?" Gabriel offers. "Then we won't get distracted by the hunters when they come out."

They return to the hotel in silence, which suits Hannah just fine.

Rain starts to fall just as they step into the lobby, thick sheets drumming against the tall windows. The room is drenched in dim light, casting long shadows across the polished floor.

"Bloody hell, it's a monsoon out there. Where did that come from?" Gabriel complains as he stares out the window. "Good thing we came back when we did. What happened to sunny California and all that?"

"So, what's the plan?" Riley asks. "Um, do you need some alone time or…"

Hannah sighs. He's directing the question to her. He might be young, but he's very in tune with her emotions and behaviors, which says more than she wants to look into right now.

"I'm sorry." Two simple words, but she hopes they hear her sincerity. "I'm off, which we can all admit we notice."

"Well, now that you mention it…" Riley has a smartass smile that he quickly wipes off when he catches her glare.

"Don't push it," Gabriel mutters, nudging him.

"I think it's this place. It's affecting me, which is unusual."

"It's the room." Gabriel's lips thin. "I don't like you sleeping in that room alone. Between being worried about you and this kid…" He points to Riley. "…sleeptalking and walking at night, I barely get any sleep."

Hannah waits for Riley to have an issue with Gabriel's statement. Instead, he grabs Hannah's arm. "Did you see that?" he whispers. He points to a shadow to the side of the hotel gift shop, a shape that flickers, almost like an opening, and then disappears as quickly as it came.

"See what?" Gabriel asks.

Riley is already moving, dragging Hannah with him, his eyes narrowed as he focuses on the spot. He runs his hand along the wood-paneled wall, and his fingers dip into a gap. A section of the wall slid back with a faint click, revealing a narrow, dark passage.

"How did you do that?" Hannah whispers, her voice wavering between excitement and hesitation.

Riley grins. "Guess we're going to find out. Come on."

They squeeze into the narrow passage, which leads them down a twisting staircase illuminated by tiny, flickering lanterns. The air is stale, tinged with the scent of old wood and something faintly metallic. At the bottom, they find themselves in front of a small, battered door with a crooked sign hanging above it: "Mr. Locke's Curiosities. "

"Mr. Locke?" Hannah mutters. "Isn't that the concierge? Seems weird he'd have his own shop, don't you think?"

"Unless it's themed related to the hotel. Can you imagine a murder room? Or a ghost room? Or a haunted room where you can buy really creepy—"

Hannah pushes open the door while Riley rambles, and as they step inside, a faint, chilling melody from an old phonograph in the corner greets them.

"Oh, freaky!" Riley exclaims in a hushed voice.

The room is larger than expected and dimly lit by orange and black string lights that cast an eerie glow over the shadowed corners. It's stuffed wall-to-wall with the macabre. Halloween masks leer from every shelf, twisted and exaggerated into grotesque expressions. There are rubber bats with sharp, glistening fangs and skeleton hands reaching out from dark corners, forever frozen mid-grasp.

The room's centerpiece is a tall glass cabinet filled with dolls, each more horrifying than the last. Their painted eyes glitter in the dim light, and as Hannah passes by, she swears the eyes move, following her as she moves farther down the room. She shivers.

One doll in particular—a porcelain figure in a crimson dress with cracked, ghostly white skin and a single, ragged eye—seems almost lifelike, her mouth open in a frozen scream, exposing tiny porcelain teeth.

Hannah will see that face in her nightmares for the rest of her life.

"This place is disturbing," Riley murmurs, leaning closer to one of the shelves.

He picks up a small clown figurine with a torn, ruffled collar and smeared red makeup. Its mouth stretches into an exaggerated grin that looks more menacing than friendly.

He turns it over and shows Hannah the small tag. "Enjoy your nightmares."

"Who would ever buy this stuff?" she asks, her voice low.

Riley shudders. "Maybe they don't have to. Maybe it buys you."

In the back of the room, tucked into the shadows, is a large trunk with rusty hinges and deep scratches gouged into the wood as if something clawed to get out. Above it, a sign reads, "Limited Edition Artifacts. Handle with Care."

Curiosity overcoming caution, Riley lifts the lid. Neatly arranged on dark velvet lies an assortment of old relics—a bone-handled dagger; a collection of vials filled with thick, dark liquids; and a large, leather-bound book with a symbol pressed into its cover.

Riley picks up the book, running his hand over the strange symbol.

Hannah looks over his shoulder at the figure resembling a mix of animal and human features, teeth bared in a horrific grin. Her finger trails over the cover, and she feels an odd pulse, almost like a heartbeat.

"It feels alive, doesn't it?" Gabriel asks softly. He's not touching anything, keeping his hands tucked inside his pant pockets. She's also noticing he's not saying much.

"Is that normal?" she asks.

He shrugs. "Could be made of human skin depending on how old it is."

"Gross," Riley says, dropping it back inside he trunk. "You're not serious, are you?"

Gabriel doesn't say anything, but from the look on his face, he knows more than he's telling.

"Maybe we should leave," Hannah whispers, backing away from the trunk.

Just then, a loud *click* echoes through the room, and they turn to see an old man standing in the doorway. His face is gaunt, shadowed under the brim of a worn hat, his eyes sunken and hollow.

"Mr. Locke, our hotel-friendly concierge?" Riley asks, his words come out more like a question instead of a statement.

The man doesn't answer, but he does smile, thin lips stretching over crooked and stained teeth. "A pleasure," he murmurs, voice like gravel. "We don't get many unexpected visitors down here." He moves forward, one slow step at a time, his gaze sliding from Riley to Hannah to Gabriel. "Everything here has a price. Some of those prices... are a bit higher than others."

Riley swallows hard. "We were just, um, browsing."

"Of course," Mr. Locke says, his eyes glinting with something close to amusement. "Feel free to browse all you like, but remember... once you leave this shop, whatever has caught your eye is yours to keep. For eternity."

Hannah grabs Riley's arm, her voice barely a whisper. "We were just leaving."

They back out of the shop, Mr. Locke watching them with that twisted smile. As they hurry up the staircase, the door slides shut behind them with a hollow *thunk*, leaving the shop and the creepy man they left behind shrouded in darkness once more.

As they return to the lobby, Hannah's nerves are shot. It feels like something left with them—a faint whisper, a shiver. Maybe they hadn't left Mr. Locke's Curiosities empty-handed.

CHAPTER
FOURTEEN

The ride up the elevator is a quiet one, and not much is spoken as they set up their high-tech ghost-hunting arsenal in Hannah's room.

"Did you have to bring everything?" Gabriel asks as he takes in all the equipment, including an EMF reader, digital thermometer, and multiple recording devices.

"I wasn't sure what all we would need," Riley says as he unpacks a few more boxes. "Where should I set it all up?"

Hannah points to different areas that have some space. It's not like there's a lot of room, that's for sure.

"Why don't we sweep the hallway?" Hannah proposes after they all stand there, staring at the devices. Riley looks proud of all his equipment. Gabriel seems bored, and Hannah just feels... impatient.

She's more than impatient to be honest. She feels unbalanced and offset and very uncomfortable being here.

"Can we talk about that room now? Like, creepy as fuck, right? All those dolls...I swear they followed us wherever we walked. And the clowns, I hate clowns, and those were beyond Stephen King, you know?" Riley prattles on while Hannah and Gabriel stare at one another.

Finally, Gabriel nods. "Not a room I want to go back in. There's something wrong with this hotel, and I think that room has something to do with it."

"Don't ask me to go back in there for a look or with our devices, okay?" Hannah tells Riley.

"Wait, so I have to go back by myself? Hell to the no, thank you very much. I'd have to be high or drunk even to consider it."

"Noted," Gabriel says wryly. "Can we go get some readings now?"

They wander the corridor multiple times with their EMF and thermometer to get readings, but nothing transmits. No spikes. No shiver in the air. Nothing.

"Maybe we should try the fourteenth floor?" Riley suggests.

They get the same results with the same empty readings. The silence between them all is louder than any ghostly whisper.

"Maybe we need to wait until it's dark?" Riley muses, hope still in his voice.

Hannah glances at Gabriel, who only gives her a shrug. "Let's take a few hours then and meet back up?" She heads toward the elevator and finds Gabriel following. "I don't need a babysitter."

He stops, holds up his hands in surrender, and retreats. "Two hours." Gabriel's voice is solid. "Check in if anything feels off."

She waves away his concern and heads to her room. A few hours of solitude is exactly what she needs.

In her room, she cleans up a little and eyes the bathtub. A hot bath sounds heavenly, and considering nothing seems to be happening in her room—no monitors are going off, no cold readings—she steps into the bathroom and turns on the tap.

Click.

She glances over her shoulder to see the bathroom door is closed. She wipes her wet hand on a towel and then wraps her fingers around the doorknob to open it. Nothing.

"Odd." She jiggles it, thinking it may be old, swollen from years of moisture, but it's soundly locked.

She takes a deep breath and reaches for her phone, except she left it on the bed. Damn it.

Knock. Knock.

She turns off the taps, unsure if she heard a knocking sound or the old pipes.

Knock. Knock. Knock.

She heard it that time. The knocking is faint at first, but the second is more desperate. The third is definitely angry.

Bang. Bang. Bang.

The door shakes, and Hannah stumbles back into the corner of the room, panic setting into her bones. Fear—real, true, basic at its core—rips through her until it settles into her lungs, making breathing hard. She pounds on her chest and tries to inhale as the door rattles with fury.

"Stop!" she tries to scream, but the fear that has taken root in her soul cages her voice so that the word comes out in a squeak.

Whatever, or whoever is on the other side, hears her, and as abruptly as everything started, it stops.

There's only stillness.

Absolute. Complete. Stillness.

Hannah edges forward, heart racing, and gently touches the doorknob. It's cold to the touch, but it turns and twists, and just like that, the door opens.

She dashes to the recording equipment and hits rewind. Whatever just happened has to be on this recording. She'll tell the guys, and they'll get to work.

Except there's nothing to hear. Just the sounds of her moving about and then the running water. No click of the door. No knocking or pounding.

Nothing.

She sinks onto the edge of the bed and leans forward, cradling her head in her hands. "Maybe I'm just tired," she whispers into the void. "But I know I didn't imagine it…"

CHAPTER
FIFTEEN

GABRIEL

While Hannah rests and Riley plays with his equipment, Gabriel joins one of the guided "ghost tours" provided by the hotel. It's a group of ten with the guide hosted by one of the front desk workers.

Why not, right? It's all for research and gives himself something to do other than twiddle his thumbs waiting for Hannah to be in a better mood. Considering he's never seen her so off before, he's been thrown for a loop. It has to be that room she's in. Whether she likes it or not, she's either bunking in with them tonight, or she's getting company in her room. Although, considering what's happened in the past in that room, having her join them on the fourteenth floor might be the smart move.

Following the tour guide through the hotel, Gabriel takes note of a few areas where the air chills and he can see his breath. Those will be good places to get some readings.

The guide drones on with the rehearsed cadence of a broken record, obviously having memorized this speech and tired of having to repeat the same words over and over.

As they're led up to the fourteenth floor, Gabriel notices how the walls, once opulent, now seem to close in around them. When the guide announces that it's rumored the ghost of a maid wanders these halls, someone makes a quip about ghostly room service and mints being left on pillows, but the laughter falls flat and is followed by a heavy silence that hangs like the cobwebs seen in the upper corners.

They approach what is called the 'infamous room' at the end of the hall, Gabriel notices Mr. Locke slipping out with an odd twinkle in his eye.

"Enjoy the show," Mr. Locke leans in close and whispers to Gabriel as they pass each other in the hall.

Show? Skepticism creeps in, and Gabriel regrets spending his time on this tour. He thought they might take their history seriously, but apparently, they bought into the dynamic of upping the ante for sales.

The guide waits until they all stand in the center. There's not much in here—a trunk where one of those freaky dolls sits, an armoire with one door half opened, a small antique makeup table with a broken mirror and a tray holding a vase with a single fake rose, and an empty perfume bottle. If they were going for ambiance, they could have added a few more things from that store downstairs.

"It's alleged that this is the room where a maid poisoned a businessman on holiday because he rejected her advances," the guide says.

Gabriel rolls his eyes. The least they can do is tell the actual truth about what happened. He's half tempted to refute the bullshit tale but stops himself. Everyone else on the tour is here for the experience. They don't care what's truth and what's a facade.

The moment the guide stops talking, lights flicker, and eerie whispering sounds fill the room. While Gabriel looks for the hidden speakers, other guest's gasps turn into guffaws. As the guide continues with his storytelling, Gabriel feels a draft swirl around him with icy fingers brushing against his skin.

"This is such malarkey," whispers a voice, ripe with scorn.

Gabriel's eyes dart from face to face to find the speaker, but everyone seems fixated on the guide.

"If only these looky-loos knew the truth." The voice is young, female, with a hint of an accent.

One of the ghosts has made an appearance but apparently only to him.

He can't help himself. "You can tell me the truth," he says softly. "I'll listen."

"Sir?" The guide stops, eyebrows arching as he pauses mid-sentence. "Did you have a question?"

Everyone turns to look at him, oblivious to what's happening around them.

"Nope. Sorry there, mate," Gabe mutters, waving him off. "Carry on."

Goosebumps rise on his arms and the back of his neck as the room drops several degrees. Others wrap their arms around themselves, pulling their light sweaters or jackets closer. They feel the cold, but they have no idea where it's coming from or why.

Gabriel looks around the room for the source of the voice. Out of the corner of his eye, he sees a young woman in a maid's uniform standing in the corner of the room. Her eyes are piercing, furious.

"Stop looking at me!" she shrieks. Her face elongates and morphs into something grotesque, and she opens her gaping jaw. Her scream fills the room, a sound no staged effect could even attempt to mimic, and she lunges straight toward Gabriel.

Heart racing, he stumbles backward, hitting his hip against a table and knocking over the flower vase. When it crashes to the floor, everyone turns his way.

"Christ!" someone exclaims.

"Did we scare you?" another guest teases, laughter bubbling up.

The guide rushes over and picks up the vase. "Are you okay?"

Gabriel ignores them all, his gaze staying fixed where the apparition had been, the echo of her rage still vibrating in his ears.

When the tour guide starts up again, Gabriel slips from the room, his heart still galloping a mile a minute. That was... unusual.

Passing through the dimly lit corridor, he makes his way back to his room. Once he shuts the door behind him, the mini bar beckons, a gleaming trove of liquid forgetfulness. He snatches a bottle, twisting the cap, and the clear liquid burns as it travels down his throat. He then pours another, trying to calm himself.

Ever since the asylum, things have been different for him. Before, there was an ease to his gift, a comfort that he knew if he touched someone, he would dive into their past. Seeing spectrals took more work... until the asylum. Now, they are everywhere, always on the peripheral until times like today, when they interact with him and only him.

Memories of the asylum claw at the edges of his mind. Sleepless nights, haunted by what he had seen... or thought he saw. The booze, once a crutch, is now a shackle he struggles to shed.

The door opens. "Jesus, Gabriel, you're white as a sheet." Riley's voice cuts through the room's stillness as he closes the door behind him. "What happened to you?"

"Found one," he grunts, eyes fixed on his empty glass.

"What? Who? Come on, man, tell me."

"The maid. She resides in that room at the very end of the hall."

Riley leans against the wall, concern etching his young face. "A real ghost?"

"Real enough to scare the shit out of me."

Silence hangs heavy before Riley breaks it again. "There's that séance tonight. We should check it out."

Gabriel nods slowly. His head is heavy, the alcohol a leaden blanket on his senses. "Call Hannah. Say it's your idea."

"Or you could stop being an ass and tell her yourself. Act like the adults you're supposed to be. I feel like a kid caught between two parents bickering over stupid stuff, you know?"

"Fuck off," Gabriel tells him, even though he knows Riley's right.

Gabriel pulls out his phone and thinks about how to word his text without pissing her off.

CHAPTER
SIXTEEN

HANNAH

Hannah's footsteps echo down the dimly lit corridor of the hotel's fourteenth floor, her pulse loud in her ears as she and Gabriel near the room where he claims to have seen the maid's spectre.

The walls seem to close in, the light fading at odd intervals, as if shadows lurk just beyond the reach of the flickering sconces, watching. She doesn't want to be here. The idea of a séance feels like tempting fate, yet Riley and Gabriel's insistence wore her down. Two against one. But Gabriel's urgency, his unnerving certainty, lingers at the back of her mind, compelling her forward.

The door creaks open, revealing the trio of amateur ghost hunters inside, waiting in tense anticipation. A musty chill hangs in the room, the air thick with the faint stench of mold and something sickly sweet, like rotting flowers.

"Took you long enough," Zach smirks, but there's an edge to his voice, a brittle confidence barely holding together.

Hannah's gaze narrows at the door. "How did you get this open?"

Sienna lifts a lock-picking kit with a grin, her eyes gleaming in the candlelight. "I'm very handy."

A warning pricks at the back of Hannah's mind—this has gone beyond mere curiosity. They're trespassing, invading a place they were never meant to be, and a sense of violation clings to her like static.

"Come on, Hannah," Riley whispers, a note of excitement laced with something else—his unspoken admiration for her, as if this would be a shared secret. She wishes it didn't affect her, but he's always had that way of drawing her in.

"Stay," Gabriel murmurs, his voice lower, raw. "They have no idea what they're dealing with, and if this turns ugly, they'll need our help."

Resigned, Hannah steps into the room, the weight of unease settling heavy in her chest. In the center of the room, the Phantom Phinders have arranged themselves in a circle, the purple candles casting flickering shadows that stretch and distort, clawing at the cracked wallpaper. The sickly scent of lemongrass oil mingles with the damp air, lending the room an almost funeral-like atmosphere.

"What's your communication path?" Gabriel asks, eyeing their haphazard setup with thinly veiled disdain.

Zach holds up a crystal pendulum, the delicate chain glinting in the candlelight. "This is our link to the other side."

"Ever done this before?" Gabriel's question slices through the room, laden with skepticism.

Zach's cheeks flush. "Once... sort of," he stammers, glancing nervously at Isaac, who rolls his eyes.

The dim light flickers, and for a heartbeat, shadows seem to coil along the floor, pooling beneath them like dark, viscous liquid. Hannah tries to ignore it, dismissing it as a trick of the candlelight, but she can't shake the sensation that something is waiting, lurking just beyond sight.

Sienna's voice cuts through the silence, her tone sing-song as she beckons Riley into the circle. Hannah watches him slip in, his face aglow with anticipation, and she feels a stab of protectiveness —if something goes wrong, they're all trapped in this room together.

Her eyes drift to the EMF reader lying on a tripod by the door, its needle still, silent. Gabriel nudges her, muttering, "I doubt it even works," but she isn't so sure.

Zach clears his throat, and his voice quivers as he speaks. "I invite Eleanor into the room to let her presence be known."

The room stills, the air growing thick, pressing in around them like an invisible weight. The candle flames shiver, casting elongated shadows that writhe across the walls. Hannah notes how the name "Eleanor" cuts through the silence, like a summons etched in steel. Naming the spirit is a focused tactic—one that could, in theory, narrow the spectral bandwidth. But as the seconds tick by, an icy tendril of doubt creeps into her thoughts.

Beside her, Gabriel stands rigid, his gaze fixed on the pendulum in Zach's hand, as if waiting for it to betray some hidden truth. The EMF remains silent, but the temperature seems to drop by degrees, a creeping chill licking at their skin.

"Are you sure you saw her?" Hannah whispers to Gabriel, feeling the pulse of dread tightening in her chest.

He doesn't look at her, his gaze fixed on the circle. "I know what I saw. And it wasn't something I could forget." His voice is low, almost haunted, and the words stir a fresh sense of unease in her.

"Alright, she doesn't feel like talking—" Zach begins to mutter, his confidence crumbling. But before he can finish, the pendulum in his hand jolts, swinging with sudden, unnatural force, slicing back and forth as though guided by an invisible hand.

Hannah's heart pounds. The movement is wrong; it's too precise, too controlled, yet none of the group is moving, and Zach's hand is steady, his knuckles white as he grips the pendulum chain. Her skepticism buckles under the chill of raw, instinctive fear. She looks to Gabriel, who gives her a grim nod, sharing her growing alarm.

"Is this Eleanor?" Zach asks, his voice barely steady. The pendulum swings back and forth in response: yes.

A nervous chuckle escapes Isaac, but it dies quickly, swallowed by the oppressive silence. Zach clears his throat, trying to mask his own fear. "Did you work here?"

Yes. The pendulum swings again, and a ripple of excitement flares in the circle, momentarily dispelling the tension.

But then something shifts, a palpable darkness creeping into the room. The air grows thicker, stagnant, as though weighed down by the presence of something far older, far hungrier, than Eleanor.

Shadows deepen, stretching up the walls like grasping fingers, and the room seems to pulse, as if alive, breathing in tandem with the fearful beating of their hearts.

"Did you kill Reginald for revenge?" Zach asks, his voice shaking.

The question hangs in the air, unanswered, but the atmosphere in the room changes—a hollow, consuming void fills the space, dragging them all into an abyss of dread.

Hannah feels an ice-cold grip on her heart, squeezing, clawing at her insides as a chill crawls up her spine, freezing her to the core. Shadows dance wildly, and for a moment, it feels as though the walls themselves are breathing, closing in, inch by inch.

Gabriel tenses beside her, his gaze darting around the room as if he can see something lurking just beyond the candlelight. "This isn't Eleanor," he whispers, his voice barely audible over the oppressive silence.

The pendulum in Zach's hand begins to spin, faster and faster, its chain a blur as it circles wildly, defying all logic. Zach's face twists, his eyes widening in terror as he struggles to release his grip, but his hand remains locked around it, the chain winding tighter, like a serpent coiling around his wrist.

"Stop! Break the circle!" Hannah's command shatters the tense silence, but her words fall into a thickening darkness that seems to devour sound itself. The shadows twist, undulating along the walls, seeping from the corners, taking on shapes that are almost human, almost monstrous.

With a sudden, violent lurch, the pendulum jerks forward, slashing toward Zach's throat. His face contorts in horror, eyes wide, as the pendulum's point slices just below his jaw, drawing a thin line of blood. He gasps, choking, as the pendulum thrashes against him, dragging his hand toward his own neck.

Gabriel surges forward, seizing Zach's wrist, wrestling the pendulum from his grasp. "Leave this circle, spirit! You are no longer welcome here!" His voice booms, cutting through the room like a blade, and for an instant, the shadows seem to hesitate, recoiling from his command.

The candles gutter, their flames nearly extinguished as darkness presses close, but Gabriel's words hold. The pendulum falls limp in Zach's hand, dropping to the floor with a dull clatter, as if whatever force held it has finally relinquished its grip.

Beside him, Sienna stifles a sob, her face pale as she presses her sweater to Zach's neck, stemming the thin trickle of blood. Isaac scrambles back, his face ashen, his eyes wild with terror.

"What... what the hell was that?" Zach gasps, his voice ragged, trembling.

Hannah places a hand on Gabriel's shoulder, her own fear churning like acid in her veins. "That wasn't Eleanor," she says, her voice barely steady. "It was something else, something... darker."

Gabriel's eyes are fixed on the shadows, his face grim. "Reginald," he mutters, his voice thick with dread. "Or... what's left of him. Whatever this place is hiding, it's more than we imagined."

A cold certainty settles over Hannah, mingling with the terror that refuses to release its grip on her heart. "Are we ready to face it?" she whispers, the weight of the question hanging heavy between them as the darkness presses in, as though the room itself waits, watching, eager for whatever horror comes next.

CHAPTER
SEVENTEEN

Hannah's hands are steady as she wipes the last smear of blood from Zach's neck, the metallic scent lingering, sharp and unsettling. "It's not deep," she mutters, more to herself than anyone else.

Relief flits through her, a brief respite in the charged air. The last thing they need is a hospital trip where she would have to explain how a séance became a near-fatal event.

Her breath trembles, but she keeps her voice even. "No hospital."

Gabriel's voice is low, filled with anger and a hint of something rawer. "That was too close, Hannah. Way too close."

The room hums with tension, the walls seeming to lean in closer, as if curious and hungry. Every surface is heavy with a dread that settles in the corners, darkening the periphery of their vision. Shadows cling to the edges of the ceiling, curling like smoke that doesn't dissipate and pressing the air down thick and dense around them. Each breath feels laced with the memory of the entity's violent intrusion, its fury staining the air.

Hannah straightens, her limbs heavy, bones aching as though drained of warmth. "Has... anything like that ever happened before?" she asks, voice barely above a whisper. Her gaze pierces the trio, who sit stunned, still forming a broken circle on the floor.

Sienna shakes her head slowly, eyes wide, her face drained of color. "That was insane," she whispers, her voice barely more than a breath.

Hannah's patience snaps, a sharp edge lining her words. "Do me a favor? Don't do anything else tonight. Whatever we called here, it's dangerous." Her gaze hardens, and she points to Zach's still-shaking hand. "That much is obvious. There's more happening here than a simple haunting. Do you understand?"

The three nod obediently, fear palpable in their hollow expressions.

Gabriel steps forward, voice gentler but just as firm. "Go back to your rooms. Keep your heads down, and if anything—anything—feels off, call us immediately."

He pulls Zach to his feet while Riley quietly gathers the remaining candles and the EMF reader, their once-blazing enthusiasm dimmed to something wary and uneasy.

Once the others finally file out, their whispers dissolving into the corridor's gloom, Hannah sags against the wall. The residual energy seeps into her bones, leaving a hollow ache and an exhaustion that cuts deeper than she cares to admit.

Gabriel studies her with a worry that hovers just beneath his stern expression. "You okay?" he asks, his voice softened.

She manages a faint smile. "Just… tired. I might crash as soon as I hit the bed."

Gabriel's brow creases, an intensity in his gaze. "This is really getting to you, isn't it?"

She laughs, a hollow sound in the empty room. "I'm fine. Really."

But even she can't deny the weight pressing down on her, an unseen hand wrapping around her shoulders and tugging her toward the ground.

Riley's voice interrupts her thoughts. "I thought… we agreed she shouldn't be alone tonight."

Gabriel's eyes harden. "She's not going anywhere by herself," he insists. "She'll stay with us."

"Oh, no I'm not," Hannah interjects, straightening as much as her drained limbs will allow. "We came here to gather evidence. I need to be in that room alone. The spirit won't come if there's more than one person." Her voice is firmer now, tinged with the calm authority she uses to quash doubts, including her own. "If anything—or anyone—visits tonight, we'll capture it on audio and video. We'll have what we need."

Riley frowns, worry flickering in his eyes. "I just don't like the thought of you in there alone."

Hannah appreciates the concern. "I'll call if anything happens," she promises, though her heart pounds at the thought. Part of her dreads what might come if she reaches out for help in the dead of night.

She finally retreats to her room. Silence settles around her, thick and watchful. The shadows seem to deepen, twisting along the walls as if to mock her supposed bravery. She hesitates at the bathroom door. The light buzzes, faintly flickering, casting her face in an unsettling, uneven glow.

"Don't be ridiculous," she whispers, a shiver skating down her spine as she forces herself to complete her nighttime routine.

Her gaze avoids her reflection in the mirror. She can't bear to look, half expecting to see something lurking over her shoulder. She jams a doorstop under the bathroom door before retreating quickly back to her bed, the unsettling feeling finally loosening its grip as she settles under the blankets.

In the heavy silence of her room, she lets her eyes drift over the equipment she set up—the infrared camera by the door and the EVP recorder glowing faintly beside the bed, all of it poised, waiting for something to happen. The quiet hum of the devices is the only noise, and it seems to amplify the silence, pressing against her ears until her heart's steady beat becomes deafening in the empty room.

Her phone pings. Gabriel and Riley have both sent her messages, reminders to call if anything feels off, warnings that somehow manage to seem both protective and pleading.

Gabriel's final message almost convinces her to go back to their room. *I don't feel right about this. Please, think about it.* Instead, she sets the phone down and burrows into the bed, hoping the equipment can stand guard against whatever hides in the shadows.

Her room seems alive with a presence, something lurking just beyond her field of vision. The silence is too thick, her own breathing too loud, the faint shadows stretching longer with each blink.

She almost wishes her brother were here, a guardian against whatever sinister force has taken an interest in her tonight. Just his presence in the corner, watching over her, would ease her nerves.

The darkness presses closer, clawing at the edges of her senses. Her own words, whispered into the void, feel flimsy, a plea rather than a prayer. "Please… no dreams," she murmurs, clinging to the edges of consciousness as sleep pulls her under, even while something waits, lurking just beyond the veil of sleep, as if biding its time to creep into her dreams and fill them with shadows of its own making.

CHAPTER
EIGHTEEN

Hannah's eyes snap open to pitch-black darkness, and a shiver of dread immediately coils in her stomach. The air is cold, damp, and alien, a stark contrast to the warmth of her bed. The stench of decaying refuse floods her senses, sour and rancid, clawing its way down her throat. She jerks upright, heart hammering, and her head throbs with a dizziness that nearly sends her sprawling. The narrow corridor around her takes shape as her eyes adjust. It's a suffocating space lined with peeling brick beside an ancient, rust-streaked garbage chute.

How did she get here?

Her mind races, every rational part of her rebelling against the scene in front of her. She's not a sleepwalker. She's never had any history of moving in her sleep, let alone wandering to a desolate part of the hotel far from her room. Panic stirs, sharp and raw, clawing at her throat. She braces herself against the frigid, crumbling wall, swallowing down the rising bile as she steadies herself, willing the sickening spin of her vision to stop.

Her breathing echoes in the corridor, loud and labored, and the oppressive silence swells around her like a heavy fog. Each slow, cautious step back down the hall feels like a journey through molasses, her every nerve prickling with a warning she can't explain.

Finally, her room greets her. Trembling, she stumbles toward the array of equipment, the screens and recording devices blinking with a mockingly tranquil calm. She fumbles with the video feed, rewinding the recording, her hands shaking as she fast-forwards through the footage. There it is, her form writhing beneath the covers, the shadows around her bed contorting in slow, haunting dances.

She starts to watch the feed, her breath caught in her throat as the blanket on screen suddenly flings itself aside, as if seized by an unseen force. There's no hand in sight, no sign of an intruder, just the blanket lifting and tossing itself away from her body.

Her heart skips several beats, stuttering. Her on-screen self sits up abruptly, her head lolling forward with a grotesque, marionette-like stiffness, and icy dread creeps up her spine as she watches herself rise, standing in a jerky, unnervingly smooth motion that defies logic, as if her limbs are being pulled by invisible strings.

"What the..." she breathes, the words hollow in the quiet room.

She rewinds and watches it again, disbelief and horror filling her gut like lead. Just over her shoulder in the recording, there's a flicker, an indistinct blur hovering behind her like a shadow that shouldn't be there, clinging to her as she's dragged upright.

Hannah leans forward, studying the footage with laser focus. Finally, she sees a pale, grainy shape, the unmistakable impression of a hand, its fingers digging into her shoulder.

The image swims in front of her eyes as she traces where that phantom grip had been. Slowly, she pulls up the sleeve of her t-shirt, and her blood runs cold.

Five faint bruises, the precise shape of fingertips, are pressed into her skin. They're fresh, darkening before her eyes, the ghostly marks searing their way into her flesh as if branded.

Her heart hammers a frenzied beat as she sets the camera down and stumbles into the bathroom, her breath coming in shallow, ragged gasps. The blinding light fills the room as she flicks the switch, and she lifts her arm up to the mirror, her shaking fingers tracing the bruises again. They look so real and vivid that she almost expects the invisible fingers to tighten, pulling her back into that darkness.

Steeling herself, she returns to the other room. Her hands hover over the equipment. She's unwilling to press play, but the need to understand, to know what happened, overrides her terror. She resumes the recording, watching as her body, slack and unnatural, slides one foot in front of the other, a grotesque parody of sleepwalking as she shuffles out of the frame. She stares as the door creaks open on its own, and a faint light blinks in the corner of the screen, marking the moment she leaves the room.

So she left the room without any awareness, guided by something unseen, but why?

Her skin prickles as she feels an insidious presence, an echo of whatever had followed her back.

Swallowing back her dread, she switches to the audio recording, recently upgraded to pick up even the faintest of sounds. The initial playback is disturbingly normal—the whirr of the fan, the faint sounds of city traffic outside, her shifting on the bed, and the soft creaks of the springs. Then, there's a hitch in the recording, a faint snort. It's an unnatural, guttural sound, almost like a strangled gasp. Her skin crawls. This must be the moment the thing pulled her upright in the video.

She listens, breath held, as her feet drag across the carpet. The door creaks open and shut, and then, there's silence. But as she fast-forwards through the final moments of the recording, an eerie hum swells, low and resonant, vibrating with a frequency that makes her teeth ache, a whispering, taunting murmur that slithers through the speakers in a language she can't understand.

Her mind races. Riley needs to hear this. He will know how to analyze the audio and pick apart the static to reveal any buried layers.

She reaches for her phone, but it's not Riley she thinks of. It's Gabriel.

When he picks up, his voice is instantly alert, a tension

threading through his words as though he'd been half expecting her call. "Hannah? What's wrong? Has something happened?"

She hesitates, struggling to find words for the terror clawing at her and the bruises darkening on her skin like malignant shadows. Her voice comes out small and tight when she finally manages to speak.

"I need you," she whispers, the words a raw plea.

There's a pause, and then Gabriel's voice, steady but strained, cuts through the phone. "I'm coming."

CHAPTER
NINETEEN

GABRIEL

Gabriel's hand traces the cold wall along the corridor outside of Hannah's room, but he's getting nothing. Not a single vibe, feel, or even a hint of a presence from the other side.

"This is where I woke up," Hannah says, her voice barely above a whisper.

Gabriel frowns as he looks down the silent and foreboding corridor. "Why here? There has to be a reason you woke up out here and not inside."

Riley shifts nervously beside them, his gaze darting to the shadows at the corners. Gabriel cocks him a side glance. What's up with the kid? Is he seeing something Gabriel can't see?

"Why don't we go back in and recheck the footage?" Hannah suggests.

She leads them back inside her room. The video plays, casting an eerie glow in the dimly lit space. Hannah's sleeping form tosses and turns before suddenly rising, zombie-like.

"I've never sleepwalked before," she murmurs, pulling down the neckline of her shirt to reveal dark marks on her arms. "And these, can you explain them?"

Gabriel leans in, his breath catching. "You were definitely visited."

Hannah shakes her head, confusion etched across her face. "I don't feel invaded or assaulted. There's no lasting menace or dread or..." Her voice falters as she looks up at him for help.

"Do you think the spirit was trying to tell you something or maybe show you something?" Gabriel's mind races with possibilities. This isn't the first time he's seen marks like this on a person, but it has been a long time. In his experience, it's never a good thing to be marked like this.

She shrugs. "Maybe. I don't know, but there's definitely something in the audio, right? I didn't imagine what I heard, right?" There's a desperation in her plea to know she's not crazy.

"I heard it too. Riley, can you bring it up again?"

Riley checks that the audio recorder is still plugged into his laptop, and then his fingers fly over the keyboard, pulling up specialized software. Gabriel watches, fascinated but lost. He has no idea how any of that shit works, nor does he really care as long as it does. Let the younger generation have their toys. He's never needed them in the past.

The kid eventually separates each sound recorded, from the hum of the fan to the traffic noises to the rustling of sheets and the ticking clock. He then somehow zeroes in and cuts out the static, analyzing it even more, breaking down all the individual sound waves until there's a single voice that sends shivers along Gabriel's skin.

"Help."

Silence.

"Stop him."

A chill runs down Gabriel's spine. The feminine voice is hauntingly familiar.

"Is that her? The maid? Eleanor?" Riley asks, wide-eyed.

Gabriel grunts and looks at Hannah, who is as pale as a ghost. "It sounds like it," he says, "but is she reaching out to help us, or does she need our help?"

"Either way, she put me in that corridor for a reason. Was it to protect me or to warn me?"

His mind whirls. Why the corridor? Why Hannah?

He has a sudden thought and holds out his hand. "Riley, give me your phone."

"Why?" Riley hands it over regardless.

"I want to look at those photos of the blueprints you took," Gabriel says.

"I can pull them up on my laptop," Riley says, taking his phone back. A few deft hits on the keyboard, and up pops Riley's photo album. He pulls up the blueprints. "What are you looking for?"

"The twelfth floor."

Riley finds the twelfth floor and enlarges it. "And then…"

"Stairwells, dumb waiters…that sort of thing. I want to see if they're connected to the floor above us."

"Ah." Riley slowly nods. "An access point. I see where you're going with this."

"Well, I don't. Can someone please explain?" Hannah sits on the bed and leans her elbows on her knees.

Gabriel leans over Riley's shoulder, his gaze darting between stairwells, dumb waiters, and… "the garbage chutes," he mutters.

"What about them?" Hannah asks.

Gabriel's heart races as the puzzle pieces come together. "They connect to the thirteenth floor. Maybe that's our access point."

Riley's eyes widen. "You mean we're going to put a hole in the wall to get to the shoot then somehow climb up to the floor above?"

"Or we find the same shoot on the fourteenth and climb down," Gabriel says, his mind churning. "It might be our only way in."

Hannah is frowning. "I don't like it," she says. "It sounds really risky."

Gabriel nods. She's right, and he doesn't know how they'll pull it off, especially in such a public place…

"So we do it at tonight," Riley says. "Quietly, discretely so no one hears us, and we'll need to figure out a way to hide the hole we make, but it's doable."

"Doable with planning, you mean. This is not something we can do on the fly, and let's be honest, we don't have time to figure it out." Hannah says, standing to her feet, hands on her hips. "There has to be another way in. All these old hotels have hidden doors and stairs, don't they? Ways for the staff to move about, right? Why don't we focus on that?"

"Good point," Riley says, turning around and leaning closer to the screen. "By the way, who's the *him* we're supposed to stop?"

Hannah's voice is barely above a whisper. "Could be Reginald."

Gabriel turns to her, surprised. "You finally believe we're dealing with a malicious spirit?"

She meets his gaze, conflict clear in her eyes. "I... I'm not sure. We need to confirm it's Reginald before I'll consider possession as an explanation for Brad's actions that made him murder his wife."

Gabriel gets that. If there's one thing he appreciates the most about Hannah, it's her willingness to take her time to get all the information before jumping to conclusions, so he understands her hesitation.

"While you guys look for another access point, I'll check out the fourteenth floor and see if I can find the chute access point," Gabriel announces even though he can't shake a growing sense of dread. What were they truly up against?

"Here, I'll send you the blueprint photos. They should help." Riley nods toward his phone.

Gabriel gets the notification that the images have been shared, nods goodbye, and leaves them in the room. He makes his way up to the fourteenth floor. As he walks down the hallway, the crimson emergency lights cast an eerie glow. His fingers trail along the wall as he measures his steps with the measurements on the blue-prints, and his heart hammers to the beat of a death drum, warning him to get out and get out now.

He ignores the warning.

His fingers draw over a slight rise in the wall. He stops and goes upward, finds a corner, and then forms a large square. This is where the garbage shoot should be.

The lights flicker above him as he takes a photo of the wall. They turn on and off, flickering unevenly. Eventually, they go out, one by one, leaving him in darkness until only the emergency red lights on the ceiling blink on, shading everything around him in crimson.

Goosebumps appear on his arms and the back of his neck. Something's happening, and he doesn't like it. He isn't prepared if he comes face to face with the malicious spirit.

He turns to head back to Hannah's room, but the corridor moves with him. It stretches, elongating until it's like he's looking through a fishbowl. Nausea and a wave of dizziness hit him, forcing him to lean on the wall for support.

"What the—"

The walls warp like a funhouse mirror. Gabriel stumbles forward, wanting, needing, to escape this hell.

"This isn't real," he mutters. "It's not real."

He forces himself to stand straight and move forward faster, running, but the fucking corridor keeps growing, moving, unending no matter how fast he moves.

Sweat trickles down his back. "Where's the bloody elevator?"

His breath comes in ragged gasps. If not the elevator, then the stairwell. It has to be close. It has to be.

Deep down, he knows none of this is real, his mind is tricking him, the spirit is playing with him, but he's frantic to escape.

Sweat pops out on his forehead and under his arms. It's running down his back, but he doesn't slow down. His breathing is labored, his heart pounding beneath his ribs. Still, he forces himself to keep moving forward even though it feels like all he's doing is running in wet cement.

Then, a quick stab of pain explodes in his chest. Gabriel stumbles, slapping a hand over his heart, massaging the area, hoping for the pain to stop, but it comes in waves, rushing over him, down his arm, up his neck.

"Oh, bloody hell," he gasps. "I'm having a heart attack."

His vision tunnels. His last thought is of Hannah and the need for her forgiveness.

Then, darkness claims him, and he knows nothing at all.

CHAPTER
TWENTY

HANNAH

The hallway stretches endlessly, shadows lurking in every corner. Hannah's heart pounds as she dials Gabriel's number one more time. It's been forty or so minutes since Gabriel left, and he hasn't checked in.

Four rings. Voicemail.

"Something's wrong," Hannah mutters, her stomach twisting.

Riley nods, his face pale. "Let's check upstairs."

The elevator ride to the fourteenth floor takes forever. When the doors finally open, the air is sucked right out of her lungs.

Gabriel sits slumped against the wall, surrounded by the ghost-hunting crew. The concierge hands him a glass of water.

Hannah rushes to his side and crouches down. Her hand grips his shoulder. "What happened?"

Gabriel waves her off weakly. "Nothing. I'm fine."

"You are not fine, Gabriel," Hannah snaps. "You're on the floor."

Zach, one of the ghost hunters, coughs. "We, uh, heard noises in the hall and then called down to the front desk when we found him passed out."

Hannah scans Gabriel's face. Sweat beads on his forehead, his shirt damp with perspiration. He looks awful.

"Do you need a doctor?" she asks, trying to keep the panic from her voice.

Gabriel shakes his head, finally meeting her gaze and giving her a pointed look. "Just need a drink and to lie down."

The concierge stands to his feet. "If you need medical assistance, please call the front desk."

"Thank you," Hannah says, dismissing him.

She takes in Gabriel's pale face and the scared looks on the ghost-hunting crews. What could have happened to him? And what was he holding back?

"Come on," Hannah says, holding out her hand to him. "Let's get you up on your feet."

Riley is there, an arm around Gabriel's waist. Together, they pull him up off the floor. Gabriel leans into Hannah, his body trembling against hers. He seems alarmingly weak.

"Let's get you to your room," she murmurs.

The group shuffles down the dimly lit hallway, the plush carpet muffling their footsteps. Riley fumbles with the key and finally manages to open the door.

As Hannah guides Gabriel inside, one of the ghost hunters calls out, "Before he woke up, he mumbled something about Reginald Blackwood."

Hannah freezes, her heart skipping a beat, but she adapts a neutral expression. The last thing she wants is those kids to put themselves in more danger. They have no idea what they're up against.

"Thank you for your help. We've got it from here."

"We can assist you," Sienna insists, eyes gleaming with excitement.

Hannah's jaw clenches. "You were injured during a séance. It's too dangerous."

Zach steps forward, his voice firm. "Six is better than three. The ghost can't take all of us on at once."

Riley catches Hannah's gaze, his expression conflicted. He

clearly agrees with Zach's logic to a point, but it's that "point" that has Hannah hesitating.

Finally, she sighs as she looks at their expectant faces. "We'll think about it, okay? I'll call you later."

She shuts the door and leans against it for a moment. The silence in the room is oppressive, like being buried under a mountain of weighted blankets.

Gabriel stumbles toward the mini-bar.

Hannah intercepts him. "You really want to drink yourself into the grave?"

His mouth opens to argue, then he stops and, with a groan, collapses into a nearby chair.

Hannah perches herself on the edge of the bed and leans forward. She can see it on Gabriel's face that something is wrong. "Now, tell us what really happened," she says, her voice soft but insistent.

With his head low, Gabriel slowly recounts his experience with the elongated hall and the suffocating dread. He didn't need to say any of the words, though. She reads it all on his face. Fear clings to him like a heavy fog.

"I swear I ran until my heart gave out," Gabriel says. "I couldn't stop. No matter how hard I tried, my legs wouldn't listen. And then…" He finally looks up, and in his eyes, there's pure fear. "Then, I just blacked out."

"You had a bloody heart attack, man," Riley says, jumping to his feet in a panic.

Gabriel makes a face, rubbing his hands over his cheeks. "Nothing as dramatic as that, mate. Just exhaustion and anxiety. This place… it's like it's inside me, worming its way into my psyche."

Hannah gives him a good look over. He's not fine, and this is more than exhaustion. With what he described and how he looks, clammy and white, he could have had a minor heart attack. He needs to be looked at by a doctor. Unfortunately, she knows he won't go. He has a thing about doctors.

Instead of insisting on something she knows he won't agree to, she heads to the bathroom, wets a cloth, and gently places it on his forehead. Her hands shake as she carefully watches him. He could have died for the second time while on her watch.

She won't let a third time happen. She can't. Taking this case on had been a mistake. She knew that from the very beginning.

What was she even thinking starting a paranormal investigation company? It was stupid and reckless, and she's blown every penny she saved up by setting them up in Vancouver. She's ruined her career and her name, and no two-bit university is going to hire her to teach anything, let alone parapsychology, not after all this.

Stick with the books and the logic, stay in her lane, and she might have made her career path into something. She knew this. She'd said this to herself over and over and over, but what did she do? She left it all behind, and for what?

She doesn't even know anymore.

Hannah's heart races, her mind churning with doubt. She runs a hand through her disheveled hair. "What was I thinking?" she mutters, her voice barely above a whisper.

Riley sits beside her and reaches for her hand, his brow furrowed. "Hannah?"

She doesn't want to look up at him and see the disappointment in his gaze. She's let him down, and she knows it. "Let's not do this."

"What do you mean?" Riley's voice cracks with distress.

Hannah stands abruptly, pacing. "This." She waves her hand between the three of them. "Why are we doing this? Risking our lives for what?" She sinks back onto the bed, head in her hands. "If it wasn't for our anonymous donations, there's no way we'd be doing this. I've used up all our money just to make sure you're taken care of," she says to Riley. "Our benefactor covers our rent and food, but that's it. I'm paying for these rooms, our car rentals, flights… and I have nothing left." She puts her face in her hands. "This was stupid," she says, looking up at Gabriel first then Riley. The disappointment on Riley's face rips her heart in half.

"Hannah, we're helping people," he protests.

She laughs bitterly. "How?" Frustration laces her words like glue. "Even if we provide some sort of tangible proof that Reginald possessed Brad to kill his wife, that's not going to get him out of prison. That's not going to bring any sort of relief to her family. In fact, that's probably going to destroy them even more because how can they have any justice with that information?"

The room seemed to close in around her. The wallpaper, once elegant, now feels oppressive. Shadows dance in the corners, taunting her.

Hannah gestures at Gabriel, her voice rising. "And you… you nearly died for nothing!"

Gabriel rises to his feet and moves toward her. He reaches out, helps her stand, and pulls her into an embrace. She resists at first then crumbles, melting into him and wrapping her arms around him. Sobs wrack her body as she clings to him like the life raft he is. Everything she's been holding inside comes out in a tsunami of tears and sobs, but Gabriel only holds her, gently rubbing her back and giving her the room and safety net to let it all out.

"Why didn't you tell me you were struggling?" he whispers, his breath warm against her ear once she manages to stop sobbing. "I would have helped."

Hannah pulls back, wiping her eyes. She wants to believe him, but actions speak louder than words, and the first chance he had, he ran.

"You were on your book tour with your fans and back to the life you'd had before. I wasn't going to ruin that for you." She steps back and gives him a slight shrug.

"I would've stayed if you'd asked."

She lets out a heavy sigh. "If there's one thing you should know about me by now, I refuse to be the reason for any resentment. Your decisions need to be made for you, not for me or Riley or any other reason."

Gabe's eyes harden with determination. "But you could have at least allowed me to make that decision."

He's right, but she admit that out loud.

"Fine then," he continues. "If you want me to make a decision, I will. Start looking for a new place, a bigger place, because I'm

123

moving in and paying half of everything. How's that for a decision?"

Riley's eyes widen while he looks at Hannah then Gabriel then back to Hannah. "Um, dude, I thought you were broke?"

Something close to a smile crosses Gabriel's face. "I was going to tell you this later, but my old publisher called me and offered me a fair amount of money for the rights of the books." His pale features whiten even more, and he sways on the spot. He retakes his seat back on the bed, obviously still weak.

"Books?" Riley asks. "What do you mean exactly when you say books?"

Gabriel nods. "It was a deal for three books. They want me to write about our cases."

Hannah doesn't know how to react or even what to say or feel. She knows one thing, though. He's not here for her. He's here so he can write these books. She looks away.

Riley is excited. "Really? That's so cool. We'll be famous."

Gabriel smirks. "Well, I don't know about famous, but yeah, people will read about you, Riley. Maybe you can finally get a girlfriend."

Gabriel looks her way, and his huge smile quickly fades. How can she be as excited as Riley? She should have known better. *He would have come back, my ass. He's only back because of the money he'll earn.*

"That's good news, right?" he asks.

There's so much being unsaid in his voice, but she knows he knows she's onto him.

"I'm happy for you," she says. "I think we all need some sleep, you especially, so let's meet for breakfast around eight and devise a plan."

She leaves before anyone can say anything back to her.

CHAPTER
TWENTY-ONE

HANNAH

Hannah collapses onto the hotel bed, exhaustion lacing every nerve, but her mind won't rest. She can't escape the memory of Gabriel clutching his chest and the look of pain that twisted his face for a split second before he shook it off like it was nothing.

"Gabriel, you stubborn idiot," she mutters, pressing her fingers to her temples. He insists it's nothing, just a bit of strain, but the image of him gasping for air, hand clutching his chest, keeps replaying in her mind.

"Moving in? He needs a doctor more than he needs another haunted house," she whispers to the empty room, curling her hands on top of the scratchy sheets.

The idea of Gabriel moving in with her and Riley gnaws at her. She wants stability, but having them both under one roof might shatter any pretense of peace she's trying to hold on to, and, let's be honest, she's used to being alone.

Still, it would solve a few practical issues. It would stretch the mysterious fund and help her make ends meet a little further if it even continues at all. Once, she thought maybe the money was coming from Gabriel, a guilt-driven, silent gesture after everything, but now, she isn't so sure.

Unable to settle, Hannah throws the sheets off, crosses to her suitcase, and pulls out a small orange bottle. The pills inside rattle, the sound unnervingly like bones clicking together as she twists off the cap. She hates these things.

The promise of dreamless sleep was always a lie. The nightmares that come with the pills aren't just dreams. They are memories, twisted and blurred by the veil of sleep, and her brother, Jake, is always at the heart of them.

Except he hasn't been around, so maybe tonight will be different.

"Please, just let me sleep," she whispers.

She tips one of the pills onto her palm and swallows it dry. The bitterness clings to her tongue as she climbs back into bed. The room darkens, something changes. A cold, creeping feeling rolls over her, like fingers brushing against her skin.

The walls stretch and twist around her, morphing into warped, pulsing shadows. The mattress feels like it's swallowing her, dragging her down until she's mummified within her own sheets.

She tries to thrash and scream, but she's suddenly somewhere else, trapped within the cramped bathroom of her room. The floor is ice-cold against her bare feet, and a sickly breeze wraps around her ankles, curling up her legs, tightening around her torso, and squeezing her in an unrelenting grip. She can't move, paralyzed against the wall.

Then, she hears it, a relentless pounding against the bathroom door.

Bang. Bang. Bang!

The noise reverberates in her skull in time with the frantic beat of her heart.

"Help!" She tries to scream, but her voice is swallowed by the air, a soundless cry.

Her fingers scrabble against the tile, fumbling until they close around a tiny pair of nail scissors stashed under the sink. She holds them up, a pathetic weapon, as the pounding intensifies. Her breaths come in short, panicked bursts.

The door splinters with a deafening crack, and a figure crashes through—a man with wide, crazed eyes and a smile stretched too far across his face.

Brad.

He grabs a fistful of her hair, wrenching her head back, and a sharp pain sears through her scalp. She claws at his hand, but her fingers slip, useless. He yanks her up, pulling her off the ground, his sneer morphing into something even more grotesque.

"You'll never stop me," he snarls, his face melting and twisting until he no longer looks human.

Now, it's Reginald, the malevolent spirit they encountered weeks ago, his eyes gleaming with vicious delight. His grip tightens, and he lifts her effortlessly, his strength otherworldly. His laugh is a haunting screech that crawls under her skin.

"This hotel will be your tomb," he hisses, his voice like nails scraping against glass.

He throws her down, and her back hits the edge of the bathtub with a sickening thud. She crumples into a ball. Pain radiates from down her spine, paralyzing her. She tries to crawl, to escape, but her body won't respond.

Reginald looms over her, a glint of steel catching the dim light as he raises a knife above her. The blade's edge gleams, and his grin widens, showing too many teeth.

"You'll never find what you're looking for," he scoffs, his voice dripping with malice. "They never do. You'll die before you learn my secrets."

Hannah's mouth opens in a silent scream as the knife plunges toward her stomach. Just before it makes contact, Reginald's face twists, morphing until he's staring down at her with Gabriel's features, a cold, twisted version of his face.

"Gabriel, please!" she begs, her voice hoarse, desperate.

But the smile on his face only deepens. "It's either you or me," he says, his eyes empty, his words hollow.

A shiver runs through her as she glimpses something behind him. A figure cloaked in white is watching from the shadows. The maid, silent and unmoving, keeps her gaze fixed on Hannah as the knife in Gabriel's hand slices Hannah's skin.

With a strangled gasp, Hannah jolts awake, bolting upright in bed. Her heart pounds wildly as she clutches her stomach, half expecting to feel the sting of the blade and the warmth of blood, but her hands meet nothing but damp, sweat-soaked skin. She's still whole. Still here. Just a nightmare.

The words repeat in her head like a mantra, desperate and calming. *It's only a nightmare. It's only a nightmare.* She steadies her breathing, running a trembling hand across her stomach, reassuring herself there are no scars, no blood.

A soft rustling breaks the silence, and her gaze darts to the corner of the room. She fumbles for the lamp and flicks it on with shaking fingers. In the dim light, a shadowed figure materializes in the chair, watching her.

"Jake?" she whispers, her heart lurching at seeing her brother's hollow eyes, his face pale and etched with sorrow.

He looks back at her, his gaze as vacant as she remembers it in her nightmares. "You're in danger, Hannah," he says, his voice ghostly, like it's coming from some distant place.

"I thought you'd moved on," she whispers, voice cracking as she grips the sheets tightly.

Jake's head shakes slowly, his form flickering like static, dissolving around the edges. "There's no peace for me, not while you're here, putting yourself at risk."

His words are like a knife twisting in her gut, his haunting gaze pinning her with a mixture of sadness and urgency. Her chest tightens. They are still tied together. She's the reason he can't move on. He's haunted by her choices.

"You don't need to protect me," she murmurs, the words barely more than a breath.

Jake only shakes his head. "The body. You need to find it."

She blinks, her mind spinning. "What body?"

His voice grows softer, almost a whisper, as his form fades even more. "Ask the woman in white." And then, with a final flicker, he's gone.

Hannah gasps, and suddenly, she's awake again, truly awake this time, the first light of dawn spilling through a crack in the curtains. Loud, insistent knocking breaks through her daze, and she stumbles toward the door.

"Hannah, open up," Gabriel calls from the other side, his words laced with tension.

She fumbles with the lock and opens the door. His eyes are wide, concern etched deeply into his face.

"Jesus, Hannah," he says, his voice rough with worry. "You look like hell. What happened?"

She lets out a breathless laugh, stepping back as they enter the room. "Good morning to you too," she mutters, running a hand through her tangled hair. "Just… bad dreams."

Riley hovers anxiously behind Gabriel, his gaze darting around the room. "Are you okay? We were worried when you didn't meet us downstairs, and when you weren't answering your phone, we rushed up here."

Hannah leans against the wall, still shaking off the haunting image of Jake, his words echoing in her mind. "I'm fine," she says, though her voice is barely steady, "but I think… we need to do a séance."

Gabriel's eyebrows shoot up. "Something did happen, didn't it?"

"You hate séances," Riley reminds her, his eyes narrowing with concern. "You wouldn't suggest that unless…"

Hannah takes a deep breath, steeling herself. "I think you're right about the maid's spirit," she says to Gabriel. "We need to contact her. There's… there's something she knows, and we won't get answers any other way."

Gabriel exchanges a tense look with Riley. "Where do we start?" he asks, his voice steady, his determination clear.

Hannah's gaze flickers to the spot in the corner where she saw Jake's apparition, her heart pounding as she remembers his final words.

"Here," she says, her voice low. "In this room."

CHAPTER
TWENTY-TWO

GABRIEL

The oppressive heaviness in the room prickles Gabriel's skin. Hannah being in this room alone is a mistake. He knew it when they first arrived, but he let her talk him into it.

If something happens to her, he'll never forgive himself.

"This is a terrible idea," he tells them as he paces the room. "Opening a pathway in here, where you sleep, isn't a good idea. Trust me on this, will you? Dreams are gateways, Hannah. You know that."

He's specifically thinking about Jake and how he is always there, haunting her.

Hannah opens the bathroom door, having changed in there. "The maid's spirit is already here, trying to communicate with me. This is our chance for answers."

"I don't like it," Gabriel insists. How many more times does he have to say it for them to finally hear him?

"So you've said," Hannah says with a shrug. "You're especially not going to like this part. I want to be the conduit."

Gabriel scowls. Damn right, he doesn't like it.

"No way. That's asking for trouble," he says.

She can argue all she wants, but he's not budging on this.

"Gabriel, you had a heart attack—"

"I did not." He has no problem denying the truth as it stares him in the face. That's all he thought about last night.

"Deny it all you want," Hannah says, "but you had one last night. What if it happens again? You won't survive. You and I both know it."

Gabriel opens his mouth to argue, but Riley speaks up. "I agree with Hannah."

The way Hannah smiles at the kid makes Gabriel grumble under his breath. Of course, he's going to agree with her. He's got a freakin' crush on her, and everyone in this room knows it.

He knows that no matter how much he argues, this woman is as stubborn as a boulder at the bottom of a creek. She's right, though. He probably did have a minor heart attack, and while there's nothing a doctor can do about it right now, he does need to be careful.

He probably should see a doctor once they're back in Canada, but he'll let Hannah argue and get him to see one. She'll get the win then.

"Fine," he growls, "but if we're doing this, then we're doing this my way. Is that clear? That means you follow my instructions. To. The. Letter."

Hannah nods.

"Before we do anything, we need food, and you need coffee." Gabriel heads to the door and opens it. Thankfully, Hannah doesn't argue, which is a miracle in itself.

***

Later, as they prepare for the séance, Gabriel's nerves are all jangled into knots. The room feels different already. Colder.

Hannah sits in a chair, her hands clasped tightly, her head bowed, and her eyes closed. He can't tell if she's sleeping, meditating, or praying.

A knock at the door has them all jump. Gabriel looks suspiciously at Riley, who races toward the door.

Gabriel glances at Hannah. She's frowning.

Riley opens the door to the group of ghost hunters. When he turns to look at Hannah, there's a sheepish grin on his face.

The kid isn't even pretending to be innocent.

"I might have let it slip what we were doing," Riley admits.

Gabriel growls.

Hannah jumps to her feet and crosses her arms. "Nope. Not happening. This is too dangerous for a bunch of—"

"Hey now, careful what you say," Zach says.

Riley closes the door after the group walks in. "They have experience," he says. "Strength in numbers, right?"

Hannah starts to argue, but Gabriel stops her. "The kid is right," he says to her. "We can't always do this alone."

"It's bad enough being responsible for…" She stops as Riley utters a complaint.

"We know the risks," Zach says. "We're here to help, and we'll follow your lead. We promise."

Gabriel steps close to Hannah and has no trouble reading her emotions. She's scared.

"Follow my lead, and we'll be okay. I've got you," he tells her.

He knows he's broken her trust and that this is asking her to take a long leap into an unknown she's not comfortable with, but it needs to be done.

Hannah sighs, her way of saying *fine*. He'll take whatever he can get.

As he looks around the room, he forces all thoughts of doubt from his mind and instead tries to see the potential in the room. There's enough power here, not much but just enough, that this might work.

Might.

As Gabriel sets up the space, Hannah is by his side, helping him. He pulls out his crystal ball and carefully places it in her waiting palms.

"This will help us lure the spirit and then contain it," Gabriel whispers, his voice soft and comforting. "The goal is to lure, contain, and then absorb."

Hannah swallows hard before she nods.

"This ball will help Hannah to draw the maid's spirit into herself," Gabriel explains to the others even though he probably doesn't need to. He's doing this more for Hannah's sake than anyone else's.

Okay, maybe for his own too.

"And then the spirit will speak through her," Riley adds, his voice catching.

Not saying a word, Hannah places the ball in the center of the salt circle they made earlier.

"Everyone, join hands," Gabriel instructs.

Gabriel is the only one not holding hands with anyone in the circle. Once everyone has settled, he rings the cleansing bell. Its clear tone pierces the silence.

"Spirit of the maid, we call to you," Hannah calls out. "Speak with us."

At first, nothing happens. Little by little, Gabriel feels a change in the air, a charge sharp enough to lift the hairs on his arms and neck. The air crackles with invisible electricity, and soon, everyone has goosebumps running down their arms.

Good. It's working.

The lights flicker ominously, and Riley gasps with excitement. "The EMF, it's going crazy!" The gauge moves slightly at first then starts to bounce around.

Gabriel's first thought is one of fear that they've gained the attention of the angry spirit again, but he doesn't feel that raw, dread-like energy from before. This energy is subtler and more feminine for lack of a better explanation.

He looks at Hannah, but her gaze is on the crystal ball, which is starting to give off a faint glow.

Yes, it's definitely working. Feminine energy or not, there's still danger, especially when it comes to Hannah. She's not trained in this. She has no idea what she's doing or what she's opening herself up to by inviting the spirit of the maid to speak through her.

Now is not the time to let fear set in, however, or to allow himself to get sidetracked.

"That's it," he murmurs as the ball grows brighter. "Come to us."

A blast of cold air whips through the room. Objects clatter to the floor.

"Direct it!" Gabriel shouts to Hannah.

Hannah stretches out her hand, and Gabriel notices how shaky she is. "Into the ball," she says, coaxing the spirit to bend her will. "We mean you no harm."

The glow intensifies. Hannah hesitates before she reaches for it—

Something pushes Gabriel from behind, and he reaches out, his hand closing around the crystal.

"Gabriel, no!" Hannah cries out.

CHAPTER
TWENTY-THREE

HANNAH

Hannah hates the way her fingers tremble as she stretches toward the glowing crystal ball. Its eerie light casts her fingers in a pale, sickly glow. She feels Gabriel's intense gaze as if he's assessing every inch of her readiness, every flicker of doubt.

This is insane. Her pulse pounds. The only reason she's even attempting this is because Gabriel, with his worsening heart condition, is in no position to conduct the séance himself.

"You need to get her into the ball," Gabriel murmurs low. Somehow, his whisper reverberates through the stillness, hollow and ominous.

Hannah nods, her throat dry as she forces calmness into her voice. "Into the ball," she coaxes, trying to project confidence and sound as though she isn't terrified out of her mind. "We mean you no harm," she intones, hoping the spirit will bend to her will. The glow intensifies in response, pulsing like a heartbeat, its light throbbing in sync with her own racing pulse.

She hears Gabriel's voice, though his lips don't move. *Touch the ball.*

She takes a deep breath, and inches her hand forward, but

before she can make contact, Gabriel's hand darts out, gripping the crystal ball instead.

"Gabriel, no!" Hannah cries, a chill surging through her. "What are you doing?"

But it's too late. Gabriel's body goes utterly rigid, his fingers glued to the sphere as though something invisible is binding him there. His eyes fly open, unfocused and disturbingly glassy.

"Gabriel?" she whispers, her heart climbing into her throat. This isn't supposed to happen. His heart can't take this. It just can't. *If he dies, this is all on her.*

Gabriel's body relaxes slightly, and he emits a strange sigh. A slow, unnatural smile spreads across his face.

"It's okay," he murmurs, though his voice has an unsettling edge. It's far too serene. "It's the female spirit. She won't hurt me." He doesn't look at her. His gaze is locked somewhere beyond, deep in the glow of the crystal. "Go ahead and ask the questions."

Hannah exchanges a nervous glance with Riley, hovering beside her, his face pale. She steels herself and takes the plunge, starting with the basics. *Establish identity* and *confirm intent.*

"What is your name?" Hannah's voice barely trembles, though she feels as if her insides are splintering. They need to know precisely who they're dealing with. Gabriel had been adamant about that.

Some spirits could deceive others and mislead them into doing things, *dangerous* things. He warned her they could summon something far worse if they weren't careful.

Gabriel's face changes, his lips twitching. Slowly, his head tilts toward her, and he jerks his hand in a sharp, commanding motion to silence her. His voice is different when he speaks—higher and edged with a hint of a New Jersey accent.

"You… you want to know about Darla?" The voice seems to crawl from his throat, thick and unnatural.

Hannah's heart races. She swallows, pressing forward, though every instinct screams to stop. "Yes. What happened to her?"

Gabriel's face contorts, twisting with pain, his eyes filling with horror. He gasps, his chest heaving with an intensity that makes

Hannah want to pull him out of whatever dark place he's ventured into.

"Oh, God," he cries, his voice trembling, his eyes staring into something she can't see. "There's... so much blood."

Riley's hand clamps onto Hannah's arm, his grip almost bruising. "Should we stop?" he whispers, his face pale, eyes wide with dread.

Every part of her screams *yes*, but she knows they might never get this chance again. Gabriel will never forgive her if she pulls him out, no matter the cost.

She shakes her head, eyes fixed on Gabriel. "We need answers." She raises her voice, steadying herself. "Gabriel, what do you see?"

His body trembles violently, a sheen of sweat glistening on his forehead. His skin is ghostly pale, drained of all color. "Reginald," he chokes out, each syllable seeming to cost him. "He's holding a knife... His eyes... they're not human."

Hannah leans in closer, her mind racing. "Where did this happen?"

Gabriel's breath comes in shallow, ragged gasps, his chest heaving. His hands twitch, and his fingers scrape against the surface of the crystal, digging into it like claws.

"Can't... breathe..." he gasps, his face turning a sickly shade.

Hannah reaches out to steady him.

He jerks away almost violently, his head snapping up as his voice, strained and distant, cuts through the air. "No! Keep... going. Won't get... another chance."

She swallows hard, trying to suppress the wave of fear swelling in her chest. "Where's Darla's body?"

Gabriel's eyes roll, their whites flashing as they move wildly in their sockets. His voice comes in short, strained bursts. "Following... Reginald. Thirteenth floor. He's carrying her..."

Then, as if a switch is thrown, Gabriel's body stiffens, his eyes widening as a low, guttural growl—inhuman and monstrous—bubbles up from his throat. The sound chills Hannah to her core.

"Something's blocking me," he snarls, his voice warped and deep, not his own. "Dark... violent..."

Without warning, his body seizes, muscles locking in place, his limbs jerking uncontrollably. Foam flecks at his lips as his back arches. Then, he collapses to the floor, convulsing violently.

"Gabe!" Hannah screams.

She drops to her knees beside him, her hands hovering uselessly, unable to steady him. His body thrashes, every muscle tensed, his face locked in a mask of pain. Riley lunges forward, grabbing his shoulders, trying to hold him still.

"Gabriel!" she cries again, panic clawing at her chest, her mind screaming in terror.

His seizure worsens, his body bending into unnatural angles, his eyes rolling back, leaving only the whites visible

Suddenly, he stills.

Hannah's breath catches as she stares down at his lifeless face, waiting for any sign of movement. She shakes his shoulders, her voice desperate. "Gabriel... come back. Please, come back."

Slowly, Gabriel's chest rises, a shallow, shuddering breath passing his lips. His eyes flutter open, unfocused and glassy. The darkness hasn't left him. His gaze is fixed on something beyond her, something she can't see.

"Thirteenth floor..." he murmurs, his voice barely a whisper, hollow and drained. "It waits... for you."

CHAPTER
TWENTY-FOUR

GABRIEL

It's been a long time since Gabriel felt anything like this, a creeping, invasive touch that slithers across his skin, tightening around him as if he's being cocooned.

The spirit enters him with an almost euphoric sensation, tingling like icy fire through his veins, pressing deep into every nerve.

As the entity settles within him, he feels a rush that is neither bliss nor pain but something twistedly close to both. His heart skips, nearly faltering under the intense pressure before stabilizing, and he knows, with an odd sense of relief, that it's the maid's spirit.

Thank God. If it had been the malicious entity that haunted Zach, he knows—*he knows*—he would be a dead man by now.

He senses her, her fear clinging to him like a second skin, her hesitation hovering between them as he tries to calm the skittish spirit within.

But even before Hannah begins her cautious questions, he's certain this spirit was once the maid, unsettled as it is. He can feel her memories flickering inside him, fractured pieces of her past bleeding into his mind. It takes her a moment to reveal her name, her voice muted with fear or perhaps fragmented by the torment that keeps her trapped. *How long has she been here, circling in fear?*

Hannah's voice cuts through the haze, steady and grounded. "Tell me what happened to Darla." She speaks softly like she's trying to soothe a frightened animal, but Gabriel feels the question land inside him like a stone dropped into a dark, bottomless well.

The maid's memories crash into him—an overwhelming flood of images, sounds, and emotions, especially raw terror. Gabriel feels himself transported, submerged in her point of view, his surroundings shifting until he is inside her body.

Inside that fateful night.

He sees through her eyes as she enters the room, where Darla's lifeless form lies sprawled on the floor, bathed in blood that has seeped into the carpet, forming dark, sticky pools that glisten under dim light. Her own heart slams against her ribs as she takes in the grisly sight. Darla's dead eyes are wide open, staring at the ceiling in silent horror.

Reginald steps into view, his face twisted with a grotesque, twisted glee, holding a blood-slick knife in his hand. His eyes. God, his eyes don't even look human, black and empty, like voids in his skull that stare through her.

Gabriel feels her fear surge, a choking, metallic taste filling her mouth as she bites her tongue, and the taste of copper floods his own senses, making him gag. He tries to push the spirit back so he can take a breath, but her panic clings to him, suffocating him, her heart pounding against his ribs like a hammer as she turns and bolts from the room.

He feels himself, or rather *her*, running, shoes slapping against the cold floor as Reginald's footsteps thunder after her, his laughter echoing in the hallway, hungry and taunting. The walls stretch and warp as she runs, bending in a nauseating, nightmarish blur that leaves him disoriented and sick. Gabriel wants to break free and push the spirit out so he can breathe again, but he resists, willing himself to stay under and keep seeing what she saw.

Then, he becomes aware of Hannah's voice calling him, her

presence dimly reaching him through the haze. She's there in the present, trying to anchor him, her hand brushing his shoulder. He's torn between two worlds, her voice pulling him back but the maid's panic dragging him deeper.

"No!" he hears himself shout, his voice ragged and strangled. "Keep… going. Won't get… another chance." He forces the words out through gritted teeth, a plea to Hannah and himself to hold on just a little longer.

"Where's Darla's body?" Hannah's asks with a sense of urgency.

Inside him, the maid's spirit stirs, her energy becoming agitated and chaotic. Images flash faster, tangled and fragmented, as she tries to show him.

Gabriel's body starts trembling as he fights to maintain control, to act as a vessel rather than let her consume him entirely. He struggles to exude calmness, but he knows that spirits, especially ones as traumatized as this, can easily slip into a rage that twists them from benign presences into malicious shadows.

The maid's voice seeps through his own, fragmented and ghostly. "Following… Reginald," she whispers, her words thin and jagged. "Thirteenth floor… He's carrying her…"

But the images in Gabriel's mind become violent, darkening to a pitch so black it feels like something else is watching him from the shadows of his own mind.

The maid's voice grows frantic, the scene slipping from her control. Gabriel senses her terror as something more powerful and malevolent blocks her vision. A low, guttural growl builds inside him, rumbling up from his chest and vibrating through his throat.

"Something's blocking me," he snarls, but the voice that escapes his lips sounds warped and monstrous. "Dark… Violent… I can't…"

Then, like a tidal wave, the energy within him shifts, flooding him with a rage so intense it's suffocating. It's as if the malevolent spirit has entered him, wrestling control, twisting, and seething with hatred and despair.

His body, overcome with the spirit's anguish, convulses. Something alien forces its way through him, clawing at his insides and filling him with emotions so intense his body can barely contain them.

Foam flecks at his lips as he falls, his body crashing to the ground with a sickening thud. His muscles spasm, his back arches, and his limbs twist at unnatural angles. For a fleeting, horrifying moment, Gabriel is paralyzed in a half-conscious state, watching through his own eyes as if he's locked inside his body, helpless, trapped in his skin while the dark entity ravages him from within.

Through the haze, he sees Hannah and Riley's terrified faces hovering over him, their mouths moving, shouting his name. He tries to reach for them, but his limbs are unresponsive, seized in the grip of an otherworldly force.

And then he feels a cold hand, thin and bony, curling around his heart, squeezing with merciless pressure.

This is it, he thinks, a flicker of consciousness breaking through. *I'm going to die.*

But as suddenly as it began, the grip loosens, the force releases him. He collapses to the floor, motionless, the room spinning, his chest heaving for air. Every part of him aches as if he's been wrung dry, his body left as an empty vessel, still and broken.

Dimly, he hears Hannah's panicked voice and feels her hands shaking him, trying to pull him back, grounding him. "Gabriel... come back. Please come back." Her voice trembles, raw with fear.

CHAPTER
TWENTY-FIVE

HANNAH

The crystal pulses with an ominous red light, casting shadows that twist and crawl up the walls like writhing tendrils. Hannah's heart thuds to a stop as Gabriel's eyes roll back, leaving only the whites visible, his body going rigid.

With a sudden, violent shudder, he collapses, hitting the floor hard. His body convulses, limbs flailing in jerky, unnatural movements as if something inside him is trying to claw its way out.

"Gabriel!" Hannah's voice breaks as she drops to the floor, cradling his head in her lap. Around her, panic flares. Riley's face has turned ashen, his hands trembling, while Sienna gasps and instinctively steps back, her hand pressed to her mouth.

"Stay calm!" Hannah commands, desperately trying to steady her voice despite fear climbing through her insides. "Everyone, stay in the circle!"

Gabriel's convulsions intensify. His fingers twist into claws, his back arching off the floor. She presses her hands to his shoulders, attempting to hold him still, but it's like holding down a live wire. She tries to breathe through the dread creeping up her spine. *This isn't how this was supposed to go.*

Something dark and malevolent has latched onto Gabriel, using him as a battlefield for a war of possession.

"Two spirits are trying to communicate through him," she manages, her voice barely concealing her rising panic. "We need to expel one back into the crystal."

Riley looks at her with wild, terrified eyes. "How do we even do that?"

Hannah has no idea. She glances at Gabriel, whose face contorts, shifting between his own and something much darker, more sinister.

"I know a way," Sienna says, trembling but determined. "I've been learning about this in my Wiccan priestess training. It might be able to trap the dark entity."

Hannah's first instinct is to dismiss it, to scoff, but she's out of options. "Fine. What do you need?" she snaps, desperation edging her voice.

"A mirror and something to draw with—chalk or charcoal. Anything that can hold binding sigils." Riley grabs her eyeliner and compact mirror from the bathroom, and Hannah strokes Gabriel's sweat-soaked hair, murmuring, "Please… please, let this work."

Sienna kneels beside them, her hands moving with steady confidence as she draws intricate, interlocking symbols on the mirror's surface, marking the four cardinal directions.

"Binding sigils," she explains. "We need to hold this in front of him. The entity will see itself, get drawn out, and be trapped by the symbols."

Gabriel's body jerks as if something inside is fighting for control. His eyes snap open, but they're empty and dark, with no trace of the man she knows. A slow, cold smile spreads across his face, one so chilling it twists her stomach.

This isn't Gabriel. This is Reginald.

Gabriel's head snaps unnaturally to the side, his neck twisting at an angle that makes Hannah cringe. She grips his hands tighter, feeling the ice-cold chill of his skin.

"Gabriel!" she pleads. "Fight it! I know you're in there."

His head jerks violently like a marionette being pulled by strings. His muscles tense as if resisting an unseen force. His hand raises, fingers curling into a fist, and she can see a flicker of Gabriel's resistance as he struggles to stop the entity from striking her.

"Sienna, hold up the mirror!" Hannah orders.

Sienna steps forward, mirror in hand. Gabriel thrashes, his head twisting away. But in the mirror's reflection, Hannah sees her—the maid, trapped within him, her eyes wide and pleading.

"Please," Hannah whispers, "help me help him."

Gabriel's body seizes, his head lurching left and right in a horrifying, puppet-like struggle. Hannah fears his neck will snap under the strain each time his head jerks.

"Gabriel," she says softly, locking her gaze with his. "Look at me. Listen to my voice. Focus on me."

His eyes, wild and feral, flicker, and for a split second, she sees him—the real Gabriel—struggling to the surface. His breathing becomes shallow and ragged, and a guttural growl escapes his throat as though the entity inside is clawing to stay in control.

Hannah's pulse races, and without thinking, she says, "I love you. I tried to deny it, but I can't anymore."

Her voice cracks, her confession surprising even herself. She's fought this feeling for so long, fearful of being hurt again, of opening herself up to the kind of pain he once caused. But now, watching him suffer, all that fear falls away. "Come back to me, Gabriel. I don't want to lose you again."

Riley releases a soft gasp, and the heat of embarrassment rushes to her cheeks, but she holds Gabriel's gaze, willing him to return.

Recognition flashes in his eyes, a spark of Gabriel fighting his way back to her.

"Now!" Hannah shouts.

Riley thrusts the mirror forward, positioning it in front of Gabriel's face. A terrible, piercing scream fills the room, so inhuman it sends a chill straight to her bones. The mirror shakes, vibrating in Riley's hands as the air thickens. A monstrous face emerges in the reflection—hollow eyes, twisted, rotting flesh—a visage that could only belong to Reginald.

The entity's scream reaches an unbearable pitch as it is drawn out of Gabriel, sucked toward the mirror. With one final, ear-splitting shriek, it vanishes into the glass. Gabriel's body goes limp, collapsing into her arms, his chest rising and falling with shallow breaths.

Sienna lets out a cry of relief, clutching the mirror. "We did it!"

But her joy is short-lived. In her excitement, she steps over the salt line, and the moment her foot crosses, a powerful force slams into her, throwing her backward. She crashes into the wall with a sickening crack, the mirror slipping from her grasp. Time seems to slow as the mirror plummets, shattering upon impact.

An icy wind erupts from the fragments, roaring through the room like a storm unleashed. Papers whip around them, furniture topples, and Hannah clutches Gabriel close. She feels the malevolent force surge past them, moving faster than she can comprehend.

The wind dies down, leaving the room in shambles. The air is heavy with an unnatural silence.

Reginald is free.

CHAPTER
TWENTY-SIX

Despite the chaotic mess in the room, Hannah focuses on Gabriel. Her hands shake as she gently pats his cheek. His eyelids flutter open. His weak smile gives her a moment of relief, quickly followed by anger that burns through her like fire.

"What were you thinking?" she hisses, her voice trembling with barely restrained fury. "Opening yourself up like that was incredibly reckless."

Gabriel manages a smirk, his hand giving hers a reassuring squeeze. "Hey, I'm all right," he whispers. "I knew what I was getting into."

Hannah's jaw tightens, the pulse thrumming in her temple. She wants to shake him and make him understand the danger he put himself in—and the fear he sent slicing through her. But her anger dims when she sees the bruises forming along his collarbone, evidence of the struggle he endured.

He did it for her.

"The thirteenth floor," Gabriel says, struggling to sit up, his face grim. "Darla's body... I saw it. Through garbage chute, that's the best way to reach her."

A sudden, sharp knock cuts through the tension, making them all jump.

Riley swings open the door. The concierge stands there, his

face calm and composed, arms neatly folded behind his back, but something is unsettling about his gaze, and his eyes don't quite meet Riley's. Instead, his head tilts as he takes in the ransacked room. The thin smile that spreads across his face is stretched just a bit too wide.

"Is everything all right?" he asks, his voice soft and even but with an edge that makes Hannah's skin crawl. "We received a complaint about some... unusual noise coming from this room."

Hannah's heartbeat quickens as the concierge's gaze lands on her. His eyes narrow. One brow lifts, and a near-imperceptible smirk tugs the corner of his mouth. His look is as cold as the draft that sweeps through the room.

"You'll clean that up, I hope," he says, gesturing to the salt, "or should I send housekeeping?" He glances at the shards of the mirror, his expression twisting into one of feigned concern. "And please, do be careful. We wouldn't want any of our... guests to injure themselves, would we?"

Riley stammers, "N-No, no, we'll, uh, we'll handle it."

The concierge's smile remains fixed, yet there's a flicker of amusement behind his eyes as if he's in on a secret that none of them are privy to. "Oh, but I insist," he replies smoothly. "I'll inform housekeeping to expect you in the dining room. We'll have something waiting for you there. A little... *hospitality* to compensate for the disturbance."

Before anyone can respond, he glides backward, disappearing down the hall with his unnatural, practiced elegance that sends a chill skittering down Hannah's spine.

The others start gathering their things, the prospect of free food pulling them from the oppressive atmosphere of the room.

Gabriel lingers behind, shooting her a concerned look. "Everything okay?"

Hannah nods, her gaze still fixed on the doorway. "That concierge," she says softly. "He feels... wrong. Have you noticed? He always shows up after these encounters."

Gabriel nods slowly. "I've been thinking that too. It's like...

he's more than just the hotel staff. Maybe a kind of... caretaker for the spirits here."

"Caretaker?" Her brow arches. "Riley keeps babbling about Salem's Lot and talking about how one becomes a vampire servant. Like that?"

Gabriel shakes his head. "It's not that exactly, but he's more than what he seems. He's connected to this place in a way I can't explain."

Hannah stares out into the hall, the prickling sensation lingering on her skin. She agrees. The concierge isn't just an observer. He's an instigator. His smile, the way his eyes gleamed with hidden knowledge, feel more like a dare than a pleasantry.

She turns back to Gabriel. "I think we need to find out what he really is."

Gabriel nods, and a flash of pain crosses his face, his hand resting against his chest where he fought for his life minutes before. She presses her palm to his chest, feeling his heartbeat and grounding herself.

"Are you okay?" Her voice softens, but her worry is palpable. "I need you to be honest with me. Whatever you went through... it wasn't normal. It wasn't safe."

Gabriel looks away, his expression distant and haunted, and he doesn't answer.

CHAPTER
TWENTY-SEVEN

Hannah's heart races as she steps into the dimly lit hotel hallway. Shadows cling to the corners, making her skin prickle. She scans for Mr. Locke, and relief washes over her when she doesn't spot the concierge's lanky figure.

He seems to be everywhere lately.

"This plan is insane," she mutters.

While Gabriel rests, Riley, Sienna, and the others are heading out to find a hardware store. They'll need heavy rope if they plan on lowering themselves down the laundry shoot from the fourteenth floor to the thirteenth.

Personally, it's crazy. It's an unstable and most definitely foolhardy plan with lots of room for error, but honestly, it is also the best and only plan they've come up with. There's no other way to access the thirteenth floor that they're aware of.

The thought of lowering themselves down the laundry chute makes her stomach churn, but they need answers. They need proof. They need something to explain the deaths plaguing this place.

The only way to get that proof is to find a way onto that floor. The malicious entity, ghost, spirit, or whatever you want to call it has to be tethered to that floor.

They need to find Darla's body to entice Reginald to show

himself so they can capture him on film. That's the proof they need, and even though it won't stand up in any court of reason, it may give the families a sense of peace.

She can't let go of the idea that there has to be at least one access point to that floor, one not readily accessible to the public but to the management. Maybe at least Mr. Locke himself has access to. No one would completely seal a floor without at least an emergency access point.

Her foot taps the floor as she waits for the elevator. The hallway suddenly feels oppressive, shadows stretching unnaturally in the corners.

She jabs the down button harder this time.

"Come on," she mutters, looking over her shoulder, feeling like she's being watched.

A soft ding. The doors slid open. Empty. She sags against the wall, keeping her finger pressed on the button that closes the doors. In some hotels, if you keep your finger pressed on it, it will take you straight to the lobby without stopping at other floors. It doesn't always work, but it does most of seven out of ten times.

Down on the lobby level, Hannah exits the elevator, and her gaze immediately goes to the concierge desk. Usually, Mr. Locke stands there, stiff but approachable in his hotel uniform, greeting each guest as they walk by.

The desk is currently empty.

"Is there something I can help you with today, Ms. Wilkins?"

Hannah glances over to find the friendly girl who had checked them in at the front desk waving her over. "Hi, actually, yes, if you don't mind. You know Mr. Ambrose, who I checked in with?"

The girl nods. "Of course, someone told me he's a famous writer."

Hannah nearly rolls her eyes. "Yes, he is, and he's actually here writing another book. About this hotel."

"Oh, that's exciting." The girl's smile is wide and genuine.

"It is indeed. I'm helping him with some research and wanted to know if you knew anything about Mr. Locke."

The girl frowns. "Mr. Locke, the concierge?"

Hannah nods. "I understand he's worked here for many years. I just wanted to know how he is to work with."

She frowns again, probably wondering how she could get herself in trouble with what she has to say.

Hannah leans in closer. "Everything anyone says to me is strictly confidential. Mr. Ambrose never reveals his sources about delicate information." She gauges the girl's interest and response to that. The expression on her face is one of disappointment. "Unless the source wants to be named in the book, of course."

"Do his books sell well?"

"Oh, yes. His last book hit the New York Times bestseller list."

Her brow furrowed even more.

Hmmm. Maybe she's too young to think the NYT list is impressive, or she might not even know what that was. Hannah isn't even sure if young people read books anymore. What were kids into these days?

"Ah," Hannah tries again, "I heard his last book went viral on TikTok?"

The girl's eyes light up at that. "Really? That's very cool." She leans forward. "Would my name be mentioned in the TikTok if I give you some juicy information?"

"If you'd like it to, I'm sure I can make sure Mr. Ambrose gives you a shout-out." Hannah doesn't like lying. Right now, any information she can get is more important than feeling guilty. And who knows? With Gabriel's book deal, it might end up in a book, and his publicity team might make videos for social media.

After looking around, probably checking to see if her coworkers are around, the girl leans on the counter, her face close to Hannah's ear. "When I first started, one of the other girls told me to stay as far away from him as possible."

"Why?"

"Supposedly, he likes to *watch* people. Especially women."

Hannah tries not to shudder. "And by watch, what do you mean?"

She shrugs. "I'm not entirely sure what she meant by that, but I've always kept my distance." She quirks her mouth a bit. "He

155

does give me the creeps. He has that *look*, you know what I mean?"

Yes. The man gives Hannah the creeps, too. There's a desperate energy, as if he wants people to find him attractive or maybe intriguing.

The girl leans in again, touching her mouth to cover her following words. "I also overheard someone say that he likes to 'collect' the tragedies that have happened here."

Hannah leans back, a little in shock. "What do you mean?

The girl shrugs. "I don't know. It's just what I heard."

"Do you remember from who?"

Was it maybe another staff member, a guest of the hotel, someone in management, or just a rumor?

The girl shakes her head. "Not really. It was like at one of our staff parties. Most of us were drinking pretty heavily." She giggles, obviously remembering something from that night.

The girl's information isn't all that helpful. It's clouded in rumors and innuendos. Hannah needs to talk to someone who has been at the hotel for a long time, someone who has known Mr. Locke, someone more her age, or even his.

Someone who wouldn't be influenced by such gossip.

"I know Mr. Locke has been here a long time," Hannah says. "Are there any other employees who have been here as long?"

The girl purses her lips as she thinks. "Gloria, maybe. She's old… older, I mean, like you. I think she's been here for over ten years or something like that."

Hannah tries hard not to be offended, considering she is probably only about fifteen years older than the girl standing in front of her. "Where can I find Gloria?"

"Down over in housekeeping. She's the manager there."

Hannah smiles at her. "Great. You've been very helpful."

"Will I be in the book?" the girl asks.

"I'll make sure you are."

Hannah leaves the lobby in search of the housekeeping offices. They aren't easy to find in the long, twisting corridors at the back of the hotel. The deeper she goes, the more aware she becomes of her surroundings. Ultra-aware might been a better description.

With every step on the thick red carpet, she feels like she's moving deeper into a narrowing tunnel. Hannah isn't generally claustrophobic, but her chest grows tighter while her heart races like she just ran up and down five sets of stairs. She stops at one point, sure that someone is either following her or watching her from one of the rooms, although every door is closed tight.

Finally, Hannah reaches the door with a small name plate on the wall beside it. *Housekeeping.* She knocks and waits for an answer from inside.

Everything is eerily quiet.

She knocks again.

"Can I help you?"

The gravelly voice comes from behind Hannah, making her startle so hard that she almost hits her head on the wall. She whirls around to come face to face with an elderly woman of about sixty. She is petite, her dark hair pulled back tight into a ponytail. Her tanned face has a few wrinkles from the sun. Looking at Hannah with shrewd dark eyes, the woman emanates a lot of intense energy. She seems like someone who has seen a lot and gone through just as much.

"Are you Gloria?" Hannah asks.

She nods. "Is there a problem that I can help you with?"

"No problem. I'm just looking for information and was told you were the perfect person to help me. It's about Mr. Locke."

The woman's eyes narrow even deeper. "Why? What has he done? Are you police?"

Hannah is intrigued. That's not a typical question to ask unless the person has a reason to make that assumption about someone else.

What is Gloria's reason?

"No, I'm not from the police. I'm actually a paranormal researcher and am here helping my colleague, Gabriel Ambrose, write a book about the hotel."

A disdainful look crosses her face. "Of course." She shakes her head. "I don't have time to talk about any of that." She turns to walk away. "I'm busy with more important tasks. The hotel doesn't run itself."

Hannah follows behind her. "I know you must be incredibly busy, but I just have a couple of questions about the hotel and the hauntings here."

Suddenly, the woman turns to give her a good glare. "You said you wanted information about Mr. Locke."

"Well, I do, considering he seems to have worked here the longest. I'm looking for some interesting tidbits about him and the hotel. Readers always want a human connection to paranormal events. Someone they can root for."

Her derisive sniff takes Hannah off guard. "Mr. Locke is not someone to root for."

Hannah's eyebrows shoot up at that.

Gloria instantly shuts down and turns away, making Hannah think the housekeeper didn't mean to say that out loud.

"What do you mean by that?" she calls after the woman.

Gloria waves a hand while shaking her head. "Nothing. I mean nothing. I'm very busy and can't answer your questions."

Hannah keeps walking at her side. "Do you believe the hotel is haunted?"

Gloria snorts. "No. It's all a gimmick to attract guests to an old rundown hotel that would've otherwise been demolished."

"So, you've never seen anything? No ghostly apparitions, no voices, no strange events?" Hannah finds that very odd.

"I've never seen anything ghostly. Not everything strange can be attributed to ghosts."

Hannah gently touches the woman's arm to get her to stop walking. "You have seen strange events though in the hotel?"

Gloria doesn't answer.

"Were you here when Brad supposedly killed his wife?"

She nods. "It was a horrible thing."

"Was that one of those strange events?"

Gloria's gaze drops, and she fidgets with the tie on her house-keeping uniform. "I need to get back to work, and you should really think about checking out soon. I think you're poking into dangerous things."

"Look, Gloria, I'll be honest with you. I'm here because there's a possibility that Brad wasn't fully in control of his actions. The victims' family asked me to investigate."

Her gaze lifts. "The victim's family?"

"They don't believe he willfully murdered his wife. They believe that he was, ah, coerced."

Gloria doesn't respond for the longest time, and Hannah thinks maybe she didn't hear Hannah or maybe she didn't fully understand what Hannah meant.

Gloria then grabs Hannah's hand tightly. "What room are you in?"

The question comes as a surprise. "The honeymoon suite. Why?"

"Are you alone?"

"No, I'm here with a few other colleagues."

"But are you alone in your room, or are you all together? Listen, regardless, you need to be careful of what you see and hear in your room."

Hannah frowns, confused. "I thought you didn't believe in ghostly events."

"I don't. Just be careful—" She stops mid-sentence, her eyes widen as something or someone draws her attention. She immediately drops her hand and straightens her shoulders. "I'll make sure that you get more towels for your room. Sorry for the inconvenience." She then quickly walks away.

Hannah slowly turns around, expecting to come face to face with a ghostly specter, but what she finds instead is Mr. Locke smiling at her from the end of the corridor.

A rush of ominous dread dribbles like slime down her spine.

Did he overhear their conversation? Did he know that Hannah has been asking about him? Will that place Hannah and her team in some kind of danger? It seems to be what Gloria implied.

There are a lot of questions that Hannah needs to find answers

159

to. It seems like ghost encounters aren't the only thing happening inside this hotel.

"Was there anything I can help you with?" Mr. Locke asks. "We don't like our guests to be down in this area. Please, in the future, ring my desk, and we will be more than happy to help you in any way we can." His voice carries down the hallway.

"Um, I went down, but you weren't at your desk." Hannah shrugs slightly, trying to convey that his presence there doesn't bother her. "I was told to come down to housekeeping, so here I am."

"Hmm," Mr. Locke says, his lips pressed tight together. "That's a little surprising to me. Which of my staff directed you down here?"

Hannah swallows hard as she pushes on the elevator button. "Oh, honestly, I don't remember. Someone I stopped in the hall somewhere, I suppose."

"Again, that is very disappointing, and I apologize. I will speak to my staff about this." Mr. Locke pulls his arms behind his back and stands stiffly beside her. "Going up?" His reedy voice sends ice through her veins.

"I… Y-Yes," Hannah stammers.

The concierge slips inside, his tall frame looming over her. His rheumy eyes fix on her face. "Enjoying your stay, Ms. Wilkins?"

"Very much," she lies.

"Encountered any… spirits?" A thin smile plays on his lips.

Hannah's throat dries up like the Sahara. "No, nothing like that."

"Pity," Mr. Locke murmurs. "The hotel has such a rich history."

The elevator crawls upward. Hannah's skin crawls with it.

"Perhaps you'd like a private tour?" he offers. "I could show you some… interesting places."

Warning bells scream in Hannah's mind. "No, thank you. As I'm sure you remember, we've already done that tour, and I'm quite busy."

"Are you sure?" His gaze intensifies. "There's so much to see on the thirteenth floor."

Hannah's breath stills in her chest, her heart thudding to a stop. How does he know? What does he know?

The elevator stops. Doors open.

"I believe this is your stop." Mr. Locke's eyes glitter with secrets as he holds the door for her.

"This isn't my floor."

"And yet, I insist you get out and perhaps take the next elevator." Mr. Locke's smirk widens. "Until next time, Ms. Wilkins."

The doors close. Hannah sags against the wall, trembling.

What have they gotten themselves into?

CHAPTER
TWENTY-EIGHT

GABRIEL

The vacuum's whine echoes down the hallway, the dull thrumming in pace with Gabriel's heartbeat. Riley's hands shake a little as he crouches by the wall, holding the utility knife he picked up at the hardware store.

"You sure about this?" Hannah whispers.

Riley nods, swallowing so hard that everyone hears the gulp. "I can do it."

He presses the blade against the wallpaper and makes a careful incision. As he cuts deeper, dust and plaster rain down.

"Hurry," Gabriel hisses.

Riley works faster, sweat beading on his brow. The laundry chute is just beyond—

A loud creak. Footsteps approach.

"Someone's coming!" Sienna whispers urgently.

Riley scrambles back as Hannah throws a canvas over the half-cut hole. They plastered on innocent smiles as a housekeeper rounds the corner.

"Everything all right here?" she asks suspiciously.

"Just fine," Hannah says smoothly. "Admiring the... architecture."

The housekeeper gives them a weird smile before she moves on. Their collective exhales of relief cause her to turn back and give them a questioning look. She mutters something in what sounds like Spanish and rounds the corner, pulling the vacuum along with her.

"That was close," Riley mutters, one hand over his chest.

They review the plan in hushed tones. They have the ropes and hooks needed to lower them down the chute. They purchase *caution* signs to leave around the area so that, hopefully, people will avoid that wall section. The plan is to return to this area at night when no one is around and hopefully sleeping, open the covering, and lower Riley and Hannah to the thirteenth floor. They will look for a door for the others to join them.

As they wrap up, Gabriel glances around and realizes Hannah isn't there. Where did she go, and when did she leave?

He heads down the hallway. When he goes to turn the corner, Hannah is there, her face pale, eyes darting nervously.

"You okay?" he asks.

"Fine," she says quickly. Too quickly. "I just thought I saw something, but I..." She glances around again. "I need something from my room."

"Like what? We have everything here."

"I forgot something."

That's all she says, and he knows he won't get anything else out of her.

She turns to leave, but Gabriel stops her by grabbing onto her arm and keeping his pressure light but firm. She reminds him of a deer caught in headlights and knows he must proceed cautiously.

"I'll come with you," he says.

She shakes her head. "That's not necessary—"

"I insist," Gabriel says, adding a full measure of firmness to his voice.

She can argue all she wants, but she's not going back there alone.

Hannah hesitates then nods reluctantly.

As they make their way toward the elevator, he catches Riley's attention and lets him know they're headed to Hannah's room and that he'll call in a few minutes. The worry etched on the kid's face creates a knot of fear in Gabriel's stomach. Hannah is off, and they both know it. What happened to rattle her so severely?

Once they're in her room, he watches as Hannah, her eyes wild as she looks around, pulling out drawers, moving picture frames off the wall, and pushing furniture away to look behind it.

"What are you looking for?" Gabriel asks, bewildered.

She pauses, hands shaking. "I'm not sure. You're going to think I'm nuts, but Gloria told me to get out. Said there was something here I shouldn't see."

Gloria? Who the hell is that?

"Are you talking about the maid ghost?"

Hannah shakes her head. "No, the head housekeeper. I met her downstairs before..." She runs her fingers on the bathroom door ledge. "She told me to leave this room, which is strange, right? Except what if it isn't? What if there's something in here I'm not supposed to see?"

"Hannah, can you stop, please? Look at me. Explain this," he begs. Her frantic exploration of the room is worrying him.

"Think about it, Gabriel. What if the ghosts aren't real? What if something else is causing all this?"

"Like what?" he presses.

She doesn't answer. Instead, she grabs a flashlight and sweeps the beam across the paintings and furniture, settling on the air vent above her bed.

Something shines in the light.

"There." Hannah points before climbing onto the mattress and peering inside.

"What is it?" Gabriel climbs up and stands beside her.

Hannah pulls her Swiss Army knife from her back pocket and unscrews the vent cover with practiced ease. The knife clatters to the floor.

"Oh my God," she whispers.

She shines her flashlight on a thin metal canister nestled inside, wires snaking from it to a small remote.

"What the hell?" Gabriel reaches for it.

Hannah stops him by grabbing his wrists. "Don't!" she says, pulling his hand away. "We don't know what it is."

"This isn't good, Hannah. There could be anything in that canister. Toxic gas? A bomb?" Gabriel's mind races, not just with all the possibilities of the danger that thing contains but also with guilt that he didn't notice it first. Worse, he didn't even think to look for it. He should have protected Hannah better. "We need to let the police know about this, Hannah."

She nods grimly then shakes her head. Is she agreeing with him or disagreeing? He has no idea.

"Give me the knife," he tells her.

"Why?"

He holds out his hand and says nothing. Either she trusts him, or she doesn't.

It takes a moment, but she hands him the knife with a decisive snip. He cuts the wires from the canister to the remote before she can say anything.

"If this is here, then other rooms must have it too," she says, her voice shaking. "We need to check everywhere."

"What's going on?" Gabriel asks. A chill creeps over him.

Hannah's eyes meet his, filled with a mix of dread and realization. "Remember my vivid dreams from the other night? I swear I talked to the maid's ghost. What if it wasn't a ghost at all but hallucinations from whatever's in these canisters?"

Gabriel's blood runs cold. It makes terrible sense, but who would do this? And why?

"We need to check your room and the laundry chute."

He nods, and they make their way to the fourteenth floor. The hallway stretches before them, dim and foreboding. Gabe's breath hitches.

"There," Hannah whispers, pointing to a vent near the laundry chute.

They approach cautiously. Hannah's Swiss Army knife glints as she unscrews the cover.

"Well, bloody hell, there's another one," Gabriel confirmed, his voice tight.

"That might be why you felt the way you did…" Hannah says as she snips the wires, her face grim. "The séance room next?"

They hurry down the hall but stop when they hear the muffled voice of a tour guide from inside. Hannah hesitates at the door.

"We can't wait," Gabriel insists, pushing it open. "We'll try to mingle with the crowd and pretend to be latecomers."

A dozen tourists turn as they enter the room. The guide falters mid-sentence.

"Please, continue," Hannah says smoothly, flashing an apologetic smile.

As the guide resumes his spiel about ghostly apparitions, Gabriel and Hannah circle the room, inspecting the vents.

"Is this part of the show?" a guest whispers excitedly.

The guide watches them carefully, uncertain whether to stop or play along.

Gabriel smiles at the man before he hears Hannah's sharp intake of breath. She found another one.

"Everyone needs to leave," Gabe announces urgently. "Maintenance issue."

The guide bristles. "Now, wait just a minute—"

Gabriel grabs his arm, speaking low. "There's something in the vent that, if released, can harm everyone in this room. Even you."

The color drains from the guide's face. He ushers the group out, his voice shaky as he leads them down the hallway.

Hannah snips the wires while Gabriel's mind races. What is happening in this hotel?

He turns toward Hannah when the door creaks open.

It's the concierge. What is he doing up here?

The moment Hannah grabs Gabriel's arm and squeezes hard, he knows she's afraid of this man. Is he behind this?

"What is going on?" Mr. Locke asks, stepping forward, his face crunched in a fierce frown.

"We've found these in the vents," Hannah says, gesturing to the canister she pulls out. "Do you know anything about them?"

Mr. Locke's eyes widen with shock. "Good Lord, no! Why would you think I was involved?" He approaches the vent, peering inside. "This is alarming. We need to alert security immediately."

Gabriel glances confusedly at Hannah. From how she approaches the man, she clearly believes he's involved, but his reaction is genuine, and he appears concerned.

Why does Gabriel feel like he walked into a play mid-act and missed out on something important?

"You know nothing about this? We found one in the vent out in the hallway and one in my room." Hannah's voice holds a brief glimmer of doubt as she confronts the man.

"This is the first I'm aware of this," Mr. Locke tells them, his voice and stance stiff. "Please excuse me while I go alert the authorities."

When Mr. Locke turns, Hannah grabs Gabriel's arm and pulls him out the door but not before Gabriel grabs a photo of the vent and canister.

The tension builds as they march down the hallway, following the concierge.

Gabriel notices Hannah playing with her phone, her fingers tapping on the screen with frustration.

"What the hell? There's no signal," she grumbles, her frustration evident.

Gabriel pulls out his phone and checks. "Same here."

Mr. Locke clears his throat. "Ah, yes. The copper wiring. Dreadful for reception."

Gabriel's eyes narrow as Hannah stiffens beside him. Something is off.

"I'll go down to my desk and make the calls," Mr. Locke offers, stepping into the elevator. He holds the door open for them, but something tells Gabriel not to enter it.

"We'll take the stairs," he says.

"Oh, thank God," Hannah says as the doors close. "I don't care what he says. I don't trust him. Do you think he honestly didn't know?"

Gabriel shrugs. "Maybe he's a good actor, but I thought he looked surprised."

She shakes her head. "No way. He's in on this."

"Should we check my room now?" Gabriel suggests, his voice low.

"You check your room. I'll head to the lobby and watch Mr. Locke."

No freaking way.

"We stick together," he tells her despite the way her lips purse. "I'm serious, Hannah. Something is going on, and I do not want you to be alone. We need to find Riley and tell him what's going on."

A chill runs down his spine, and he swears they are being watched.

As they approach his room, Hannah stops and pulls back. "There's something I need to do first. Check out your room, and I'll be right back."

Gabriel shakes his head. "No way."

"Honestly, Gabriel. We already took care of the canister. My room is safe now. I'll be five minutes, tops." She glances at her watch.

He doesn't like it but knows he can't stop her. "Five minutes, and if you're not back, I'm coming to you."

"Deal."

Hannah retreats. Once she pushes the door to the stairs open, Gabriel feels something kick him in the side, like a sucker punch, and he doubles over with pain, but she's already gone, the door closing behind her.

What the hell was that? He whirls around, but he's all alone in the hallway now. He holds a hand tight to his side and breathes through the pain.

"*You're a dead man,*" a voice whispers in his ear.

CHAPTER
TWENTY-NINE

HANNAH

Hannah's eyes snap open. Darkness. Cold. Pain throbbing in her skull.

She groans, pushing herself up on shaky arms, and looks around. Dust and cobwebs cling to her clothes, and an ancient sign on the wall reads "Thirteenth Floor" in faded letters.

What the hell?

"Where am I?" she mumbles, her mouth dry and bitter.

Where is everyone else? She tries to peer through the black, but she barely sees anything beyond where she's sitting.

The last thing she remembers is getting into the elevator to go to the lobby to call the police.

She pushes herself up to her feet, her hands going to the wall for support as everything spins around her.

"Hello?" Hannah calls out, her voice echoing. "Is anyone there?"

A chuckle comes from behind her, low and eerie. She whirls around.

There's nothing there.

"Over here," a voice taunts from in front of her.

She spins again. Nothing.

Hannah's heart races. What is going on?

"You think you've figured it all out?" Mr. Locke's voice reverberates from everywhere all at once. "You don't know anything."

"Where are you? Why are you doing this?" Hannah demands as she touches her pounding head.

She stumbles down the corridor, desperate for an exit, but with each step, the hallway stretches out, appearing twice as long.

"This isn't real," she tells herself, breaking into a run. "It's just a hallucination."

In her head, she knows this isn't real. Whatever is happening to her is because of whatever chemical Locke has been using, but the musty air in her lungs feels real. The pounding of her feet sounds real. The pulsing in her chest, making her heart race, is very definitely real, so much so she feels like she's going to have a heart attack.

Is this how Gabe felt before he collapsed in the fourteenth-floor corridor?

She comes to a door and tries to open it, but it's locked. So is the next and the next.

"You can't escape, Dr. Wilkins," Locke's voice mocks. "Your precious science can't save you now."

Hannah speeds up but only passes a few more doors before she needs to slow down and catch her breath. She needs to be rational and calm and not freak out. All of this is a chemically induced reaction, and her mind is playing tricks on her thanks to whatever is in the air.

She knows this, and yet, she can't get rid of the sense of panic, her anxiety growing. Is she going crazy?

No. She's not. There is a rational explanation for what's happening to her. She knows this.

And yet, the corridor keeps stretching endlessly before her.

Hannah's fingers tremble as she grasps another doorknob. Locked. Like all the others.

"Come on," she mutters, moving to the next door. One of them has to be opened. Why lock all the doors on a floor no one can access?

Her scientific mind races, analyzing what kind of chemical can induce hallucinations and sensory manipulation. There are too many to name, too many that could have been used on her, on Gabriel, on the others...

Hannah slumps against the wall, chest heaving. "Think, Hannah," she whispers. "What's real? What's the plan?"

The laundry chute. They were going to use it to descend to this floor and find the body. If she could just find that chute, she might be able to escape.

She closes her eyes, visualizing the hotel's layout. She opens her eyes, turns, and returns to where she started, dragging her hands along the way, feeling for the dip where the laundry chute should be.

"Come on. Where are you?"

She walks by a room, but the sound of a door opening slowly, the creaking of age echoing all around her, stops her.

"Don't," she tells herself. "It's not real."

It's just another hallucination. She needs to ignore it, stick to the plan, and find a way out of here and back to Gabriel and Riley. They must be worried sick about her by now.

But her curiosity—the same drive that led her to parapsychology—takes over.

Hannah turns toward the open door. Although she can barely see inside it, she does the one thing she knows she shouldn't do.

She steps inside.

The door slams shut behind her.

"No!" She whips around, wrapping her hands around the doorknob, and yanks on the handle, but it's locked. It won't budge. "Let me out," she screams, banging her fists on the hardwood paneling.

A light blooms behind her. Hannah turns around to see the room magically transform to what was probably its formal glory.

It's a big suite, and all the furnishings look new and pristine, not aged like those in her room. The area rug is fresh, and the walls are a soft gray color that flickers with the cracking fire in the fireplace. There's a table to the side with two half-filled wine glasses, an open bottle between them.

"This isn't real. This isn't real," Hannah chants out loud, hoping the sound of her voice will break whatever spell she's under.

It doesn't.

She walks toward the table when she passes by a mirror. She slowly turns and looks—not at her reflection but at Darla's face. At Darla's features.

She glances at herself and, through the mirror, sees that she's wearing a simple, soft yellow dress with flounces and ribbons. With slow movements, Hannah raises one hand and gently touches her hair, her fingers curling around the tight chignon. It feels so real.

It is real.

"How…" she breathes.

In the mirror, a man approaches.

Reginald.

CHAPTER
THIRTY

GABRIEL

Crawling on his hands and knees, feeling like he just had the shit kicked out of him, Gabriel makes it to the elevator and manages to pull himself up. Thank God it's empty.

He presses the button for the twelfth floor and sags against the wall, holding tight to his side. He can't get the eerie voice calling him a dead man out of his head. Who was that? It was a voice he hadn't heard yet, a voice he didn't recognize but one full of authority.

What the hell is going on with this place? It's time to stop playing games and time to kick some ass rather than have his get kicked again. All he needs to do is get to Hannah's room and get to work.

Enough is enough.

Except when he gets there, she's nowhere to be found. What is there, though, is her wallet and phone, lying discarded on the ground. What the hell?

After hobbling over to the bedside table, he calls the concierge desk.

"This is the concierge. How may I be of assistance?" a feminine voice, older and not one he's spoken with yet, asks.

"I'm looking for Mr. Locke," Gabriel says. If anyone knows where Hannah is, it's that man, and if he's around, then he knows Hannah's okay.

If he's not...

"Oh, I'm sorry. Mr. Locke is off shift now. Is there anything I can do to help?"

Gabriel hangs up, grabs Hannah's things, and heads upstairs without answering. When he bursts through the door, Riley sits there, playing on his computer, his headphones covering his ears.

"Hey, man. I wasn't sure where you guys went. Listen, I've been doing some playing around and—"

"Hannah's gone," Gabriel interrupts. "I think Locke took her."

"What do you mean? I just saw her." His forehead furrows as he drops his gaze back to his computer.

"Riley, I'm serious."

For all the times the kid has been playing games on his computer, now it is not.

"So am I. I just saw her in the hallway outside her bedroom." Riley twists his computer screen to show Gabriel. "See? I was able to hack into their cameras. Do you know they monitor everything? It's creepy. I mean, they don't watch people in their rooms, but all the hallways, elevators, corridors, staff rooms... Even that room with all that freaky haunted stuff."

Gabriel collapses on the bed, hand still pressed tight to his side.

"What's wrong with you?" Riley gives him an odd look. "Seriously, mate, you look as knickered as a horse plowing into a barrel."

Gabriel snorts then grimaces at the resulting pain. "That bad, huh? Well, I had my ass handed to me by a ghost out in the hallway, believe it or not."

Riley points toward the door. "Out there? When?"

Gabriel shrugs. "Ten, fifteen minutes, maybe? Not sure to be honest. I kind of blacked out for a minute or more."

Riley shakes his head as his fingers do whatever they do on his keyboard. Then, he turns the monitor around for Gabriel to see. He watches himself jerk and then falls to the floor.

"Looks like you tripped," the kid says. He plays the video back.

Yep, it sure looked like he tripped, but Gabriel knows he didn't. He was punched, pushed, and then threatened.

"I didn't trip. Someone, or something, punched me in the side." He lifts up his shirt, and sure enough, a bruise already formed.

"Shiiiiittt, that looks like it hurts," Riley says, giving a sharp whistle.

"No fuck." Gabriel gently touches his side. Nothing seems broken, but it hurts like a mother.

"There's no one else in that hallway with you, though. You're saying a ghost hit you? That's bat shit crazy talk right there."

"And yet, it happened. Some ghosts can take corporal form if they're strong enough."

"But there's nothing there…"

Gabriel shrugs. "It happened. Back to Hannah, please. Where the hell is she? I was just in her room, and she's not there."

"No, you weren't. Dude, I have the camera looking at her door right here, and I've been keeping an eye on it for the last hour or so. Hannah went in, but she hasn't come out. Have you tried calling her?"

Gabriel pulls out her room key and phone from his back pocket. "Look harder because I was just in there, and these were lying on the floor."

"What the…" It takes Riley a few minutes before he glances up with fear and confusion. "I'm seeing nothing. Like, not even you going into her room. You weren't even on that floor or elevator, I swear." He buries his head as his fingers move a mile a minute. "Unless… Shit, they've got it looped."

"What?" Gabriel's heart races as he stands beside Riley and watches the video over the kid's shoulder. Sure enough, you can see where it's been looped. "What the fuck?"

"When did you last see her?" Riley asks.

"Shit. The vents. That's why I'm here and why we split up. We found canisters in the vents in the hallway on the fourteenth floor and in that room with the hauntings. There's some type of hallucinogenic in the canisters."

With Riley giving him a *what-the-fuck* type look, Gabriel explains Hannah's theory about the canisters, the hallucinogenic gas, and the fake hauntings.

There's a knock on the door. Hoping it's Hannah, Gabriel opens it to find the Phantom Phinder trio. They walk in.

"Guys, you need to hear this," Riley says, his voice leveling up with excitement. "We've all been gassed, literally."

Zach snorts. "What are you talking about?"

Gabriel explains it once more as the trio stands there with dropped jaws.

"Holy shit," Sienna says. "Are the canisters still there?"

Gabriel nods. "Mr. Locke said he was going to contact the police, but he's off shift now, and Hannah is missing."

"Whoa, dude, way to bury the lead. What happened to Hannah?" Zach shakes his head and rushes to the door. "You fill the others in, and I'll check out those canisters."

"Don't touch them, and check any vent you see," Gabriel warns him.

"Photos only. Got it. This is fucked up, man, seriously," Zach says before the door closes behind him.

"So while we were in there, holding that séance, we were just hallucinating?" Sienna clarifies, her eyes wide.

Gabriel nods. "Possibly."

"So the hauntings, they're not real?"

"No, that's not what I'm saying." Gabriel sighs. "The hauntings are real, but what we experienced and to what level... that I don't know. Until we figure out what's in the canisters, it's all just a guessing game."

Riley shuts the lid on his laptop. "Zach shouldn't be in that room alone," he says as he grabs a bag and leads the way out.

They all head to the supposed haunted room where Zach is snapping photos of the canister.

"I don't feel well," Sienna mumbles, holding her stomach.

"I think we're okay. We snipped the wires," Gabriel tells her, dismissing the girl. These kids are just getting in the way. He needs to find Hannah.

"So it's a type of hallucinogen, but what kind…" Riley muses. "Has to be stronger than nitrous."

"Psilocybin?" Zach suggests.

Gabriel frowns. "Mushrooms?"

Zach shrugs. "Could be spores," he says. "Sprayed remotely. Make people see things. They do it in clubs."

Gabriel tells them about the canister found in Hannah's room.

Riley's eyes are saucer round. "Oh my God. Brad could've hallucinated," he says. "This could help his case, right? It could be the evidence we need to exonerate him."

Gabriel nods grimly. "His lawyer could push for an appeal at least."

"So now we just need to find Hannah. We should call the police." Riley says, pulling out his phone.

"Locke took her to the thirteenth floor," Gabriel says.

Riley pauses mid-dial. "How do you know that?"

"Hannah." Gabriel shrugs. "She's been watching the guy and believes he's behind everything. Even those," he says, pointing to the canisters. "Someone obviously took her and probably drugged her to get her out of her room. Who else would know how to get down to that floor?"

"So, how do we get down there?"

"First thing first, someone needs to call the police." Gabriel glances at the ghost-hunting trio.

"On it." Sienna pulls out her phone, dials, and holds it up to her ear, walking a little off to the distance.

Knowing that's taken care of, Gabriel marches does the hall-way, grabbing the fire extinguisher from the wall. Using the bottom of it, he hits it on the area they cut earlier. It doesn't take long for the plaster to fall away, revealing an old wooden sliding door.

"Yes!" Riley almost shouts.

Gabriel smiles, relieved that they are this much closer to finding Hannah.

It takes some muscle to open the door.

Riley leans inward and confirms that it's the chute. "You're not going to fit, though," he says, pulling himself out of the opening and eyeing Gabriel's mid-drift. "I'm going down," Riley hands Gabriel the rope. "Tie this around me, will you?"

Gabriel's fingers fumble as he struggles to knot the rope. Zach is there, holding his hand out, not saying a word. It doesn't take Zach long to make some kind of knot before slapping Riley on the back.

Gabriel's stomach flips and flops as Riley climbs into the chute, feet first. The kid takes a minute to situate himself before he gives Gabriel the nod to lower him. He starts to, but then the rope slips in his hand.

"Hey, watch it!" Riley cries out.

"Sorry," Gabriel mutters as he gets a better grip on the rope and continues to lower Riley.

It's probably a good thing the kid is the one going down and not him...the rope probably would have broken, or he'd have gotten himself stuck in there.

Gabriel's palms sweat as he lowers the rope, Zach now helping him with the weight.

"There's a board across the opening," Riley yells up. "I think I can—"

They hear a bunch of thuds and grunts before there's a crash, and the rope goes slack in their hands. Gabriel looks down the chute and can barely see Riley waving up at him.

Then, they hear a scream.

Hannah's scream.

Gabriel's blood runs cold.

CHAPTER
THIRTY-ONE

HANNAH

Hannah's heart pounds as Reginald charges at her, knife glinting in the dim light.

"You money-grubbing whore!" he snarls.

She dodges, just barely. His bulk belies his speed, and his rage makes him strong and surprisingly agile.

Hannah sprints across the room for the door, but it's locked.

She's trapped. Her chest constricts as Reginald runs at her again, the knife in his hand raised high. He brings it down just as Hannah sidesteps and shoves him away.

The knife slams into the wood, quivering with the impact.

"This isn't real," Hannah pants, racing across the room. "I'm hallucinating. There has to be a canister somewhere in this room."

If this is a hallucination, then he isn't real. A sense of calm hits her, and she spins to face him, standing her ground.

Except he looks real. He sounds real. The spit flying from his mouth and spraying her body feels real.

Shit.

The maid suddenly materializes behind Reginald, her arms waving wildly. "He's real! You need to move out of the way!"

Shocked, Hannah does more than just move out of the way.

Her martial arts training and self-defense courses take over, and she kicks, hitting him solid in the kneecap.

As Reginald stumbles past the mirror, she gasps.

That's not Reginald. That's Mr. Locke.

"What the hell is happening?" she demands.

While Locke tumbles to the ground, there's a shout in the hallway. Suddenly, someone bangs on the door. It bursts open, and Gabriel rushes in with Riley behind him.

The second Gabriel enters the room, his eyes roll back.

The maid has possessed him.

Gabriel hurls a heavy chair with inhuman strength, throwing it at Reginald. It hits the hearth, and the bricks start to break apart. Gabriel picks up the chair again and smashes it against the hearth once, twice, three more times.

Smash. Smash. Smash.

The bricks crumble into a pile of rubble and dust, and out falls a skeleton.

A skeleton wearing the same dress Hannah is wearing.

"Darla," Hannah whispers, horrified.

Gabriel drops to his knees and gathers the bones into his arms.

The space around Gabriel flickers, the air shimmers, and time warps as Hannah sees Gabriel. Then, Darla's features morph into one, separate, and morph again.

Reginald convulses and drops to his knees, his hands cradling his head as he bends over in pain.

Hannah watches, frozen, as Reginald's spirit tears free.

Mr. Locke screeches as Reginald's ghost twists and turns in the air until he finally implodes into himself and vanishes into nothingness.

A chill settles into the room, and the shimmering from earlier glows bright before it fades, and all they see are the dusty floorboards, rotting wood, and cobwebs draping from the corners. A rat scurries past, its nails clicking.

Hannah glances down at herself, expecting to see the old dress, but she only finds her dusty jeans and ripped sweater. Her hands glide over her knotted hair, and she sighs with relief.

She's herself again.

"Gabriel?" Her voice trembles as she sees him still cradling the skeleton, knee-deep in debris with tears streaming down his face.

A wisp of ethereal light simmers, and the maid's spirit hovers over Gabriel's body and the skeleton, one hand reaching out before she slowly floats away, disappearing through a boarded window.

Hannah sinks beside Gabriel, wrapping her arms around him. "It's over," she whispers.

There's pounding out in the hallway.

"Umm, guys...." Riley calls out, a little frantic.

Any light from the hallway disappears as shadows fill the space where the door once stood. Two police officers stand there, hands on their holsters, stern frowns on their faces.

Riley edges between them, eyes wild. "Hannah? Gabriel? Are you okay? I brought some help. That's the guy that kidnapped her," he says, pointing to the collapsed body of Mr. Locke.

***

The lobby buzzes with tension and relief, echoing footsteps and hushed voices swirling around Hannah and Gabriel. He lays on a stretcher, hooked up to a few monitors.

Mr. Locke's face is grim as he is led away in handcuffs, his shoulders hunched under the weight of his secrets. His gaze darts around, landing on Hannah just before he is escorted out the glass doors.

She looks away, her focus snapping back to Gabriel, whose complexion is pale and strained.

Riley is there, busying himself with worry. "The police are going through everything. They found a collection of videotapes the concierge kept hidden in his office," he says, lowering his voice. "They watched one, and it was... it was a murder, Hannah. Someone was killed here years ago, and he had it all on tape. And..." He glances around before leaning in closer to add, "There's a good chance he has the footage of the night Brad killed his wife. This could be the break we need."

Hannah's mind races, a tangled mix of horror and hope.

She reaches for Gabriel's hand, and he tenses under her touch. "What's wrong?" She glances at the paramedic and then at the heart monitor.

"Sir," the paramedic says, his face grim, "there was an irregularity in the reading. I'd feel better if we took you in for observation."

Gabriel is about to wave him off. She watches as his mouth forms a polite but firm refusal.

She gives him a headshake, tightening her grip on his hand. "You're going," she says, her tone leaving no room for argument. "Don't bother arguing. I'll be right there with you."

Frustration and vulnerability war in his eyes, and she's almost positive he's going to refuse, but then he relaxes and gives a resigned nod.

"Thank you," she whispers, leaning close and kissing his forehead softly.

"Ma'am, unfortunately, you will need to follow us," the paramedic says as she walks with them toward the ambulance.

She nods to Gabriel, promising to be there soon, and then watches as the door closes and the vehicle leaves.

"What can I do?" Riley asks, standing beside her.

She sighs before running her fingers through her hair, trying to work out a few of the knots. "Guess it's time to pack up our things and check out," she says, her voice softened by exhaustion. "It's over. For now, anyway."

Riley nods. "I'll take care of it. Ah, the police found all the canisters, every one except..." His face clouds for a minute. "There weren't any of the thirteenth floor."

Hannah pauses, that strange detail settling over her. "That doesn't make any sense," she says.

Riley shrugs.

"How did you get down there anyway?"

"We found the chute. Gabriel lowered me on a rope, and then I found a hidden staircase. Sienna thinks it's one of those servant staircases from back in the day. There's a secret door just off a corridor at the end of each hall."

"Crazy," she says. "I'm glad you found it and then found me in time." She pulls Riley in for a hug. "Otherwise, Mr. Locke would have killed me."

Riley eventually steps back, his face a little redder than before. "Yeah, well, we made a promise to each other, remember? Back at Ghost Asylum. Like I was going to break it and let something bad happen to you."

"Excuse me, ma'am, but we're ready for your statement. Yours too," an officer interrupts and points to Hannah and Riley.

"I want to head to the hospital to make sure my friend is okay," Hannah says. "Is there any way we can do this later?"

"Unfortunately, we have a lot of questions that need to be answered," the officer says without apologizing.

"I'd like to know how they managed to solve a decades-old case in just a few days," another officer says, just off to the side. "Have you looked them up? One of them is an author. I bet this makes it into a book."

As Hannah and Riley are led off to separate corners to give their statements, they share a smile. If only those officers knew...

CHAPTER
THIRTY-TWO

HANNAH

The sharp antiseptic smell fills Hannah's nose as she takes in Gabriel's small hospital room, its sterile walls and unforgiving fluorescent lights pressing down like an unwelcome weight.

Despite the cool blue view outside, the room closes in, a confinement in its own right. She would hate it if it were her lying in that hospital bed.

Attempting a gentle smile, she nudges the spoonful of grayish mush toward Gabriel. "Come on. You've gotta eat something," she coaxes, trying to sound cheerful.

Gabriel eyes the spoon with exaggerated disdain. "That's not food, Hannah. That's punishment. I'd rather face another night in that hotel than eat the shit they call hospital food."

She rolls her eyes and lets the spoon clink back against the tray. "Believe me, I wish we were somewhere else too, but this was the best I could get from the cafeteria." She hesitates then adds, "I could ask Riley to grab a few smoothies before he leaves."

Gabriel looks at her with surprise. "Is he heading home?"

"Not yet, actually. He's taking a little holiday." A hint of a smile plays on her lips. "With Sienna."

Gabriel's eyes light up. "Riley? With Sienna?" He chuckles, the familiar spark of humor returning to his face. "Good for him. She's a good kid and more his age. Hopefully, this means he'll let go of his puppy love for you," he mutters.

Hannah smiles, though something twists slightly in her stomach. As happy as she is for Riley, they still don't know the others very well.

"This is what he needs," Gabriel says, reading her mind. "The kid deserves an escape, even for a little bit. I doubt things will last, but you never know. And besides, this gives you and I some time to ourselves once we get back to Vancouver."

"You and I aren't going anywhere anytime soon," she reminds him as he shifts in the bed, glancing toward the door. "Doctor's orders. I know you're itching to get out, but you're staying here until they're sure you're okay."

Gabriel sighs, looking frustrated. "This is costing a fortune, Hannah. I'll be fine to fly home. Let's just go."

Before she can protest, a soft knock interrupts, and Andrea, Brad's sister-in-law and technically their client, slips into the room. Her face is a mix of worry and relief. Her eyes immediately find Gabriel's, and they fill with unshed tears.

"I'm so sorry," she whispers, moving to his bedside. "I can't help but feel this is all my fault." Her hand gently brushes his arm, as if she wants to reassure herself he is okay.

Gabriel gives her a comforting smile. "It's nothing, Andrea. Just a little blip. They're keeping me here because they're bored."

"Are you sure?"

"It's going to take more than a little ghost to scare me into the grave. Trust me," Gabriel tells her then looks toward Hannah.

Hannah steps forward, holding a slim file and memory stick she protected in her bag. Riley had the smarts to record everything he found while breaking into the hotel's security system.

She hands them over to Andrea, her hands shaking slightly. "For your lawyer. Everything we found… about your sister, about those hidden vents. It might just be enough to give you and your family some closure finally."

Andrea's eyes shimmer as she looks from the file to Hannah.

Without a word, she pulls her into a hug, holding on tightly. "Thank you. I don't know how to repay you for this."

Hannah closes her eyes briefly, feeling the weight of Andrea's gratitude and the pain they all share. "Just… take care of yourself. And don't lose hope for Brad."

Andrea nods and gives Gabriel one last concerned look before she slips quietly from the room.

Silence lingers as Hannah watches the door close, feeling the moment's significance. Then, she turns back to Gabriel, her mind drifting to the words she said when she thought he was going to die on her, but then she changes her mind. Now isn't the time.

"So, this book about the hotel," she says instead, trying to lighten the mood. "All the so-called hauntings… they weren't exactly ghostly encounters, were they?"

Gabe leans back, a wry smile on his lips. "More like the twisted work of one very disturbed individual. But people love a good ghost story. Throw in a serial killer, and we might just have a bestseller."

Hannah chuckles, the weight on her shoulders momentarily lifting. "Well, the truth of the thirteenth floor can wait," she says, a spark of mischief in her eye. "We'll let people believe in the hauntings for now. We've earned a little bit of peace after all this."

"We'll eventually need to break it down, though. That was some weird shit, Hannah, and not all of it was drug-related."

She nods. "I know, but maybe we'll leave that for another day. Let me unpack it first here." She points to her head then to her heart.

Something passes over Gabriel's face, and she swears he's going to bring up the things she said, the things she wasn't sure he heard her say.

"As long as we do it together, okay?" he asks. "I meant what I said about moving in. And don't think I will let you backtrack from your declaration either."

There's a challenge in his gaze, one that she's not sure she's ready to meet.

Hannah pulls out her phone and pretends to scan her emails. "Oh, look… We might have a new client."

She gives him a soft smile. He holds out his arm and pulls her close as she climbs onto the bed and snuggles in.

"You're ready for a new haunting all ready?" Gabriel asks with a yawn. "So many ghosts, so little time to write about them…" His voice trails off, and Hannah watches him as he falls asleep.

She scrolls through her emails for real this time and finds one from their mysterious benefactor, proof he or she isn't Gabriel.

She opens the email and gasps as she reads the message, her heart sinking with fear.

Until next time… in The Haunting of Blood Manor, coming soon.

JOIN ME

I'm just going to throw this out there. There will be more books, but while you wait, why not join me over in my VIP ADDICTS Subscription group?

What happens over there? A lot.

For instance, the next book in this series, you'll read early chapters there. Plus, you'll read all patient confessions before they're published. Plus, you get to name characters. And you get free books.

It's also a better way to stay in touch rather than a mailing list that you may or may not see in your inbox.

https://patreon.com/jacksteen

Click to check it out. No pressure, but if you do sign up, be sure to say hello in one of the posts, and I'll raise a toast to you at the pub.

WHO AM I?

(Hey, you, don't skip this part. Important info about this book at the end, even if you already think you know who I am.)

My name is Jack Steen.

I write the Asylum Confession series.

And now I'm writing this Haunted series.

I don't go online much. You won't see me on social media often unless I have something to tell you about the books, and it's very rare that I answer any emails or DMs that come my way about my books or me or anything else. It's not that I'm being rude (well, maybe…) but it's more that I appreciate my privacy, and I think you can understand that.

Thanks for reading!

MORE BOOKS?

Hell yes.

Head to my website and sign up - www.jacksteenbooks.com and join my NEWSLETTER

Or, if you want to become an Asylum Addict, join my VIP ADDICTS SUBSCRIPTION GROUP, where you'll get to read whatever I write for free and before anyone else and even get some free stuff.

http://patreon.com/jacksteen

Turn the page to find out about the next book coming your way!

THE HAUNTING OF BLOOD MANOR

Next Book in the Series is: The Haunting of Blood Manor

Coming soon…

THE ASYLUM CONFESSION SERIES

The Asylum Confessions: The Originals

This is the first book in the Asylum Confession Series and full of my favorite confessions to date.

Word of Warning: you'll become addicted to the confessions you read … so get ready!

These books are available as ebook, paperback, hardcover and even audio. Check out my website - www.jacksteenbooks.com for all the details on how to fill your latest addiction!